CONNO[ ]
DIAMOND

MICHAEL CLAXTON
&
ROSALIE ENSTROM

Copyright © 2021 Rosalie Enstrom & Michael Claxton

All rights reserved.

ISBN: 9798764360140

CONTENTS

Acknowledgements   Page 7

Prologue   Page 9

Book 1   Page 11

Book 2   Page 82

Book 3   Page 125

Book 4   Page 181

Book 5   Page 214

Epilogue   Page 243

The Authors   Page 247

ACKNOWLEDGEMENTS

To Angela Claxton for Editing the manuscript.

Russell Perry of Russell Perry Digital Marketing,

for his technical support.

DEDICATION

To the Fellowship of Australian Writers Queensland,

who battled on against all odds to present the

The Readers and Writers Festival 2021.

To the committee, members, and presenters,

enthusiastically led by the President,

our good friend Jim Higgins.

CONNOR'S DIAMOND

Prologue

Kabul, Afghanistan, Sunday 13th of August 2017.

IT WAS A MASSACRE.

The six-man patrol had been lured into the derelict remains of the hospital on the outskirts of this God-forsaken wilderness. It had been bombed by ISIS a week earlier. The informant had reported that there was a group of children trapped in the basement.

Two soldiers stood guard in the doorway as the Lieutenant led the others and cautiously entered the building, They followed the stairs to the lower ground floor, drawn by the sound of a child crying.

He noticed the wire and tape recorder.

But before he could say "Bomb!" there was an almighty explosion, dirt and dust came bellowing from the building.

The two guards immediately covered their faces and raced down through the smoke-filled corridors to the aid of their comrades; only to find three corpses, and the Lieutenant's mutilated body; he was barely alive.

With an arm each, they dragged him up the stairs to the light of the entrance; there they were met with a hail of bullets. One of them returned the fire, whilst the other attempted to stop the flow of blood from the dying officer, at the same time screaming into his radio for help.

It was ten long minutes that seemed like a lifetime before the whirling sounds of the rescue team's helicopters could be heard.

By this time, there was only one survivor: Lance corporal Connor Malloy. The Lieutenant had died in his arms, and his colleague killed by a sniper's bullet.

Malloy's injuries were superficial; and soon healed, however the ghosts of his past would never leave, and haunted him for the rest of his life, eventually driving him into a world of insanity.

***

Book 1: The Discovery

Chapter 1

Brisbane, Queensland. Monday 6th March 2023.

"Wake up Connor!"

I was awoken by a loud bang on the door, and a shout from the other side.

I rubbed away the gunk and grubs from my eyes, and through the blurry mist, slowly raised my head and viewed my surroundings; four grey walls, toilet, washbasin, and a door with a spyhole.

I had a thumping headache and a mouth like the bottom of a filthy bird cage; God I felt awful, and had no recollection of the day before, or why I was here.

The door opened and the uniformed officer entered. The Senior Constable was a large friendly man who handed me a carton of coffee.

"Buck up mate, you're in court in a couple of hours. We can't have you looking like this in front of the Magistrate, now can we?"

"Cheers cobber," I thanked him, then sat up and took a slurp of the lukewarm drink.

"No worries, now get yourself cleaned up." He left the room, closing the door behind him.

I stood by the sink looking into the small mirror; he was right, I looked like shite.

Bruising around my eye, congealed blood in my nostrils and beard. I filled the sink with cold water and sunk my face into it, in an attempt to revive myself; it was not working!

There was a small window set high in the cell wall. I could see the dark clouds, and hear the wind whistling through the tree tops. I guessed we were in for another storm; I mused as I dried my face.

My thoughts were interrupted as the door swung open.

"Come on Connor, it's time to go."

Two hours later I was led into the dock, before the arrival of the Magistrate.

"All stand in court," called the usher…….

"Mr Van Vuuren." The magistrate sighed, looked up from the notes, removed her spectacles and stared me in the face.

"Mr Van Vuuren." She paused and lowered her tone. "Connor; this is the fifth time over the past year that you have been before this court. Once again I've read all the social reports and your old Commanding Officer has given up his valuable time to attend and outline your impressive list of commendations." She gave another sigh of exasperation.

"This has to be the last time; my hands are tied. The next occasion, should there be one, will most definitely result in a custodial sentence. We cannot tolerate your drunken brawling in the city. We sympathise with the Vets who have served their country and appreciate the difficulties of readjusting to civilian life. But you, Connor, have refused the support that has been offered and have immersed yourself into a life of drinking and drugs. I implore you to take the help that is being offered. Your problems will not go away by themselves."

I resignedly raised my head and looked at her through my blurry bloodshot eyes, as she replaced her glasses to pronounce sentence.

"I will conditionally discharge you for the next twelve months. However, should you be brought before me again, along with any other offences that you have committed, this one will have to be taken into consideration. Is there anything that you wish to say?"

"No, Ma'am," I replied in a whisper.

"Then this case is closed." The court stood, and she retired to her chambers.

Outside the courthouse, I shook hands with Major Mike Simpson and thanked him for coming to my aid.

"Do you have time for a quick beer?" I tentatively enquired, knowing that on the last occasion he had given me two fifty-dollar bills, and I had hoped that this might prompt him to do so again.

"Are you serious Connor? Did you not listen to anything that the Magistrate said?" replied the Major in disbelief.

"Just one for old time's sake," I begged.

"Hardly old time's sake! It was only two months ago that we were walking out of the same courthouse," he reminded me, as his face reddened around the neck. "I'll not be buying you a beer. All that I am prepared to give you is exactly the same advice as the court: either pull your shit together or look forward to time in the clink!"

"Bbb, but" I stammered, as I tried to think of an appropriate excuse for my behaviour.

"But nothing! Just look at yourself, man. Once I would have described you as a proud, handsome upright figure in your Lieutenant's uniform, but now? Just look at yourself."

He grabbed my arm and pulled me towards an adjacent shop window.

"Look, tell me what you see," he argued.

The Major was right, the reflection in the window did not lie; my life on the streets had taken its toll. My blood-shot eyes; an unshaven, dirty face drawn and scarred; shoulder length hair matted and unkempt. Yes, I looked a pathetic sight. I slovenly, stood with my shoulders drooped, in clothes that had been neither washed nor ironed for a week. Standing alongside me was Simpson, an officer in uniform immaculately turned out, all of which reminded me of what I had once been; my eyes welled up.

He sighed and placed a sympathetic hand on my shoulder.

"Wipe your face, Connor. Lift up your chin. Yes, life is hard, but whoever told you it would be easy? Giving you a handout will not solve your problems. All combat soldiers carry scars and suffer nightmares. If you really want them to go away, take the help offered to you. There's no shame in reaching out for support." He handed me a card with the details of a counselling group, the same card that he had offered me twice before; then glanced at his watch.

"Sorry, I've got to go."

I stood there as he disappeared into the pedestrian traffic. I wanted to scream at the patronising bastard and tell him to fuck off! But the words stuck in my throat; everything that he had said was true.

I choked back the tears and dejectedly slouched off in the opposite direction, back to the Brisbane bedsit that I shared with Alex, another Veteran; but at least he had a job.

I searched the small apartment in the hope of something strong to drink but had to settle on the one tinny left in the fridge from the night before. Then ferreted through Alex's drawers hoping to find his stash of weed; there was none, so I relit the remains of a spliff from a dirty ashtray.

Neither the beer nor smoke helped to change my foul mood. I struggled to recall the events of the previous day, unable to remember what had started the fight; one minute I was having a few drinks, the next minute in a tussle with the bouncer, who was trying to eject me from the bar….

….. then nothing.

That was until I woke up in the Watch House, charged with being drunk and disorderly.

"What the hell have I become? Thirty years of age and I can't even remember what happened yesterday." I cried aloud, my anger turning to self-pity.

Eighteen months earlier, they discharged me from the Australian Army on medical grounds; ten years in Special Services had taken its toll, and the nightmares had begun.

"Lieutenant Connor van Vuuren, many times decorated for bravery under fire, admired by friends and colleagues, not to mention my adoring mother and sister. What would they think if they could all see me now? A coward that is too scared to front any of them."

This habit of talking to myself, is it another sign of my insanity?

My nerves were shot; the last tour in Afghanistan had pushed me over the edge.

I had lost more colleagues and friends. Despite every patrol being met with smiles from the locals, I was in fear of putting a foot out of the camp, afraid of being shot in the back by a sniper or treading on a booby trapped mine. My enemy wore no uniform, so I never knew who was a friend or foe, or what lay behind a smiling face?

Sleep deprivation had become a serious problem, endless sleepless nights. And when sleep came the same recurring nightmare. Me standing over the motionless body of a Taliban fighter who lay there grinning up at me; I continued to pour more and more bullets into his body, but his grin widened, and he refused to die.

Each night, the Arab haunted me, and it drove me deeper into a world of insanity. My only escape came from the inside of a whisky bottle or smoking substances that transported me into a better world.

The Medical Discharge? I didn't like it but was exhausted and could not fight the decision of the authorities.

I was too embarrassed to return to my family, despite them constantly haranguing me to do so; putting them off with lies, lies and more lies. "Everything is ok; the new job starts next Monday; I have to visit a sick friend; I'll visit as soon as I can," the excuses and apologies just kept coming.

It was now time to give up the struggle and admit defeat. It's been eighteen months of sliding deeper into the abyss of self-pity. The Major was right. It's time to man up and face the family, although the thoughts of confessing all to mother and Jess are filling me with more than a little trepidation; I'd rather be facing the Taliban.

The decision made, it was a shower, then a rummage through the drawers to find whatever clean clothes I could, packed them into my old army rucksack and headed for the coach station, but not before sending a brief text message to Alex.

Heading up north to the family. Thanks for everything.
Connor
PS, sorry for nicking the last tinny out of the fridge. Have borrowed a few clean shirts from your wardrobe, will replace when I get sorted.
Cheers, Connor

It was dark when I boarded the coach.

There were only a few other passengers, so I stowed my baggage, snuggled into a seat at the back, closed my eyes and attempted to sleep, knowing that it would be a long journey; sixteen hours north to Townsville, then another bus for the four-hour trip inland to Burgville, where I would be met by Jessica, that is, if her old Beetle was still road worthy. Finally, another two-hour drive until we arrived at the Clover Sheep Station.

I could not sleep as we sped north along the highway. It was time that I could have spent planning my future, or at least preparing acceptable excuses for mother for when I arrived. But no, it was not to be and when I closed my eyes, all I could see was that fucking Arab grinning back at me. Sleep would never happen, despite the rhythmic motion of the coach as it cruised through the night.

My mind went back to memories of my first visit to Burgville.

As children, we had been accustomed to a good life, living in a large house in the suburbs of Brisbane. Father had a well-paid job as a mining engineer, a fly-in fly-out worker. He was away for a month at a time, whilst mother was devoted to her life of running a spotless home and bringing up two children.

At thirteen, our idyllic world was brought crashing down. There had been a collapse in the mine shaft, twenty men trapped, and father had been one of the dozens that failed to survive the fall.

After the accident the owner denied all liability, there was a protracted court case which the company won, consequently there was little by way of compensation. The following two years were miserable, as mother struggled to pay the mortgage and eventually, we were threatened with eviction.

In desperation, she replied to an advertisement in the newspaper.

A gentleman farmer in Burgville required a live-in housekeeper, and would happily consider a widow with children, if they were all fit and healthy.

They exchanged telephone calls and correspondence over the next few months. Then we were packed and heading north in a removal lorry containing little other than mother's prized possessions.

The 'Gentleman Farmer' was Patrick O'Brien. His family had emigrated from Ireland in the 1950s. He was not totally unlikeable, but full of the blarney and prone to exaggeration. The Clover Sheep Station had not had sheep on its land for many years. The lush meadows that he had described were fifteen and a half thousand acres of scrubland, with little in the way of grass. When he had taken over the farm from his ailing father in the 1990s, he sold off the last of the sheep and became a Grazier and currently had a thousand head of cattle.

It was hardly the dream that mother had envisaged, but he was a kind man, and they were married two years later. Patrick had battled hard to win over Jess, and with his Irish charm, he eventually did so, although no one would ever replace our father.

Farming in central Queensland could never be described as easy. Patrick was a hard worker, but barely turned a profit, always praying for the rain that never came and constantly moving the cattle in search of patchy areas of edible grasses.

Both Jess and I had become accomplished riders and were expected to assist with droving the cattle. As teenagers, we naturally did a fair bit of moaning and groaning, but we loved nothing more than being in the saddle. They were happy days that only ended when I enlisted in the Army.

Thoughts of those good times comforted me, and my eyes slowly closed. I got some sleep, knowing that I would soon be home and back in the saddle.

Two hours later, I was abruptly awoken by the driver.

"Hoy, you on the back seat. Unless you want to go to Cairns mate, you'd better move your butt."

I rubbed away the sleep from my eyes and yawned. We had stopped at the bus station and most of the other passengers had already got off, so I grabbed my rucksack and scrambled off before it pulled away on the rest of its journey.

6.00am, the bus station was getting busy with commuters making their way to work. My coach did not leave until 8.00am, so I had time for a wash and some breakfast.

I bought my ticket to Burgville and sat in a nearby café. Maybe I should buy some flowers or other gift, it had been two years since I had seen any of them. But when I looked inside my wallet, all that I had to my name were two twenty-dollar bills, hardly enough to cover the coffee and sandwich that I had just ordered, so skipped the idea of presents.

We passed through the green hinterland, then the White Mountain National Park, the landscape rapidly changing from green to brown and the heat of the sun beating down hard upon the bus; thank God the air conditioning was working.

Stepping off the bus, I looked around and instantly saw Jessica on the far pavement; she waved from a distance and excitedly dashed across the road towards me. Suddenly, she stopped in her tracks; her smile disappeared.

"Connor?" she asked in disbelief. "What's happened? You look awful. What in hell's name have you been up to? You look like shit!"

"Thanks Jess, that's quite a welcome," I replied, trying to make light of her comments. She might have been shocked at my appearance, but her reaction certainly knocked me back.
This was not the welcome that I had hoped for.

We stood there, tears forming in our eyes. She then threw her arms around my neck and hugged tightly; she nearly squeezed the life out of me.

"It's a long story. I'll tell you when we get home."

"I don't think so! Mother would have a heart attack if she saw you looking like that. There are few shops in the village, thankfully though there is a hairdresser; we need to get you cleaned up before going to the farm."

Two hours later, my hair was washed, trimmed and my stubbly beard removed.

"That looks much better." She then handed me a pair of jeans that she had bought from the Op Shop, whilst I was being tidied up in the salon. "These might not be designer labelled, but they are clean and should fit." She said with a smile.

The first hour of the drive from Burgville passed quietly, the superficial, meaningless conversation filling the old car as we bumped our way along the narrow roads, leading us out into the wilderness. Then Jessica pulled onto the roadside and switched off the engine.

"Ok, let's have it. For the last couple of years, you have been feeding mother all this bull about leaving the Army for this wonderful new job. If half of that is true, which I very much doubt and by looking at the state of you, your new employers cannot be paying you much. So, let's cut out all the crap and tell me what has been going on," she demanded.

Jessica was two years older and had always been the sibling with the authority. There was no point in lying to her.

I told her the full story. The medical discharge, nightmares, the bouts of drinking and drug abuse, even being dragged before the courts frequently. There was no way of denying that my life was a mess.

By the time that I had finished, my eyes were red raw. I felt ashamed and sick to the pit of my stomach and expected a damning rebuke, but she gently placed her arms around me, pulled me to her, and lovingly kissed me. The last time she had done that was when I was a thirteen-year-old and we had received the news of father's death.

"Don't cry, Connor, you're nearly home. I promise you that this is nothing we cannot mend. We will get you sorted; it will just be like the old days."

She wiped my face with a tissue, turned on the engine and continued the drive home.

It was dusk when we arrived, the redness of the sun sinking below the mountains in the distance, the farmhouse aglow with soft lights. Mother and Patrick were standing in the doorway with beaming smiles.

Hugs, kisses, and handshakes.

Mother's only concern was wanting to know why I had lost so much weight in two years.

"Come in. Dinner's nearly ready. Looks like I'll need to feed you up!" she said as she dragged me into the dining room.

Yes, it was good to be home!

***

Chapter 2

During dinner, mother and Patrick bombarded me with questions, wanting to know all about this new job and what I had been doing with my life since leaving the army.

I immediately went into autopilot and spewed out the same old lies. A hard kick met this on the shins under the table from Jessica, who was sitting opposite me. Then she glared me in the eye.

"Brother; I think you need to change your story."

"Whatever do you mean?" asked mother.

"I think Connor has something else to add; don't you brother?

My sister always referred to me as 'brother' whenever she was annoyed; it was time for me to stop the lies and confess that there was no fantastic new job, and that they had discharged me from the army.

I was filled not only with food, but with embarrassment. My head dropped. I pushed away the half-eaten plate and recounted the sorry tale that I had told to Jess earlier.

Mother was near to tears; she had never wanted me to join the army in the first place.

Patrick was enraged and his anger poured out; not directed at me, but at those who had treated me in this way.

"The bastards! Love you when they need you and throw you out when they don't: bloody typical of this government." He was a simple farmer and had no time for either the military or others in positions of authority.

"You are home now; no more nightmares and busy noisy cities, just the peace and tranquillity of the farm; we'll soon have you fit and well," mother assured me.

"Yes, and when you're recovered, there is plenty of work here. You'll soon be back in the saddle," said Patrick with a comforting smile.

Now who's telling lies? I thought. They were struggling as it was, without having another mouth to feed. They could not have shown more support, which only made me feel even more guilty, now wondering just how much of a burden I was going to be.

My story had been told, so I excused myself from the table and went to my old room where I collapsed on to the bed. Drained from the long coach journey, and the disclosures about my mental state.

The room had not changed since my last visit some three years earlier. The smell of the freshly laundered bed linen had a soporific effect as I buried myself beneath the sheets.

I was home and knew that I would sleep well as my eyelids closed.

3.00am. and Jess burst into my room.

My body soaked in sweat, eyes wide open and screaming at the ceiling fan that had been slowly turning.

"Die! For God's sake, why won't you die!"

"Shush, shush," she lay beside me and turned my head towards her. "It's ok, it's ok." She reached out for the towel that was beside the bed and wiped my face. "He's gone, there's no one there, he's gone," she lovingly assured me.

I could not stop shivering, not knowing whether it was the nightmare or a fever. Jess dampened the towel from the sink and pressed it to my forehead, then snuggled beside me. The shaking subsided, my eyelids closed, and I returned to sleep, held in my sister's loving embrace.

In the morning I awoke to silence; it was 9.00am, I could hear no noises from the other rooms, so I pulled on my shorts and one of Alex's shirts and peered out of the bedroom door. I took one sniff, then followed the smell of bacon that was coming from the kitchen.

"Did you sleep?" mother asked as she stood at the hob.

"I think so," I quietly replied, as I struggled to recall, not being sure whether Jess had come to my room, or whether it was just another dream.

"Where is everyone?" I tentatively enquired.

"We don't keep city hours here," she said with a grin. "They left before six, moving the cattle. Hopefully, they should be back before dusk."

Now I felt the pangs of guilt, I thought it was still early; back in Brisbane, I was rarely out of bed before noon.

After breakfast, I helped mother to gather in the first load of washing. We then sat on the deck with a coffee.

"So, what are we going to do with you?" she asked.

"In what way? They shoot horses, don't they?" I replied.

"Hilarious, I'm glad to see that you've not lost your sense of humour. But seriously, Jess told me you had another bad turn last night; you are still my child and I need you to get better, so how are we to go about it?" she asked in earnest.

I thoughtfully stared into my coffee; so, it was not just another dream. Jessica had nursed me through the night.

"I don't know. They offered me counselling in the early days, but like an idiot I refused, in the belief that drink was the answer, I now know that it is not!"

"Let's put that behind us. It's time to start again." She took another sip, then put her coffee down. "When your father was killed, if it had not been for having you two, I might have gone down the same road. Luckily, I was never much of a drinker, so instead lost myself in my books. I found reading to be such an excellent therapy, losing myself in some fantasy world away from reality and the pain."

I could see her eyes lighting up, dragging me into her world of literature, and being my mentor would also take her out of the tedium of being a farmer's wife.

"I'm prepared to give it a go. Surely it can't do any harm," I sarcastically jibed, then tried to remember the last time that I had held a book in my hand, probably not since school.

The back wall of the living room was covered floor to ceiling with books; the most diverse range imaginable, from Charles Dickens to J. K. Rowling and everything in between.

"So, what do you like to read?" she eagerly asked.

"I don't know. What would you suggest?"

"Well, you must have read books when you were out in Afghanistan."

I could hardly admit to my mother that the only reading material circulating around the camp was pornographic magazines.

"Not really. What do you suggest?"

She pawed through the shelves, then pulled out half a dozen books. The one that caught my eye was a novel by Wilbur Smith, "The Power of the Sword", set in South Africa.

"Why that one?" she asked.

"Well, it has an eye-catching cover and I've actually heard of Wilbur Smith; unlike the other five. And I remember you telling me tales of Grandpa Joseph who lived in South Africa."

I took the book back out onto the deck, sat in the rocking chair, and started to read. An hour later, mother broke off from her chores and came out to see how I was getting on.

"What, not finished yet," she teased, then asked if I'd like another coffee.

"In ten minutes, I just need to finish this chapter," I replied, without raising my head from the novel; the story had gripped me and I did not want to put it down.

It was late afternoon when I finally closed the book. Mother had been right; an excellent book is a great distraction from reality.

I stretched my body, which was stiff from having sat reading all day.

Then I saw the four figures on horseback, slowly approaching from the distance.

Jess and Patrick, plus Charlie and Keon, the two hands that lived in the shed out back. They were all tired, dirty, and dusty from the day's work, each one dying for a cold beer and a shower, but not before unsaddling and washing down their horses.

I embarrassingly stood by watching; I'd forgotten how hard it was on the farm, and what a full day's work involved; certainly not sitting on my arse reading a book!

"Sorry I wasn't up in time to come and help," I pathetically tried to explain to Patrick.

"Don't be daft Connor, we need you fit and well before you get back into the saddle; sleep is the best cure for most things, so get as much as you can." Spoken kindly and sincerely and delivered with a gentle smile by the affable Irishman.

An hour later, we were all sat around the dining table.

Charlie and Keon had been invited in, as was the normal practice after a long day in the saddle. It was good to see them both again. Two cheery characters, their forefathers, had been on this land since time began.

When we had first arrived at Burgville, they had been the first aboriginals that I had ever spoken to; I had never met any in Brisbane and distrusted anyone that did not come from the city. Unlike my sister, who brazenly flirted with the two cowboys.

It became a different story once they had taught the pair of us to ride. Jess had decided that at twenty-nine and twenty-six, they were too old and lost interest in them. The more I got to know them, the more I became fascinated by their indigenous background.

"So brother, while we have been working our butts off, what have you been doing with your time today?"

Harsh, I thought; what happened to all the concern and compassion from the night before? And……. 'We will get you sorted; it will just be like the old days.'

The old days? Really?

Upon reflection, I guess it was. Little had changed and although we were older now, she still believed, that as the senior, she would always be the one in charge.

During the next seven days, I had read five more novels, eaten a mountain of mother's meals, taken my first tentative ride on Buck; a fresh horse that had been aptly named. Most importantly though, I had only suffered two more nightmares, enjoying the benefits of five nights' undisturbed rest.

After dinner on the eighth day, we sat around chatting about my reading choices. Typical boy stories; action and adventures, with a male hero winning the day.

Jess, of course, was the first to criticise my choice of reading material and asked if I had read 'Flight to the New World'. It was a historical memoir by Catherine van Niekerk, an elderly second cousin who lives in Perth.

"Memoirs? How boring!" I replied with an exaggerated yawn.

Mother then rebuked me for being so disrespectful; Aunt Catherine had spent years in research and writing the book. Jess then fetched it from the shelves and unceremoniously dumped it on my lap.

"Try this one for size, dear brother!"

Not for the first time since my return, I had to apologise and promised to read it in the morning.

I couldn't recall my father's sister, Aunt Cath, who lives in Perth; we had visited once when I was a small child, but that was many years ago. I guess if a member of the family had taken the time and trouble to write this massive account of our family history, then the least I could do was to read it. What else did I have to do with my time.

***

Chapter 3

I was always taught that you should not judge a book by the cover, and this is a perfect example of that old saying.

"Flight to the New World" weighed a ton and was bound in an unimaginative cover. I thought it would take me a lifetime to battle my way through it, as I dutifully turned to the first page.

On July 19, 1769, the ss Spiering, a Dutch India Frigate Class Ship, built and owned by the Dutch East India Company, arrived in the Cape, South Africa. On board, Pieter van Vuuren, born in Sas van Gent, Zeeland, Netherlands. He was a soldier in the VOC service at nine gulden per month, a free Burgher and tailor by trade.

The voyage was not without incident. Of the crew and 200 passengers who sailed, 52 died, either at sea or in the makeshift quarantine camp at the Cape. The first death was a small child, David Oosthuizen, whose eight-month-old, shrouded body, gently laid on a plank across the bulwark from where they tipped it into the sea as the ship's bell pealed and the passengers assembled on the deck singing hymns at his funeral. As the days turned into weeks and weeks into months, there were many more such funerals carried out. Typhus took the lives of many men, women, and children. Pieter van Vuuren, however, did avoid this disease.

Once settled in the Cape, in a lavish ceremony, he married Katrina Oosthuizen.

In 1771, he bought Oranjeplassie from Johannes van der Merwe, a fruit and vegetable farmer, for the sum of two thousand gulden, which his family then owned for a century. Oranjeplassie would later become an affluent residential suburb on the slopes of Table Mountain above Reservoir, and named after the sight of the abundant orange trees growing in Table Valley. It belonged to the Castle of the Cape of Good Hope; not only the first building built in the Cape but also built as a unique five rampart stone castle.

Dirk van Vuuren, born in 1781, was the only son of Pieter and Katrina and, after the death of his father, he and his wife Wilhelmina continued to grow oranges, other fruit, and vegetables. He also became involved in the Burger Council, of which he was a member. Their first child, Pieter, named after his grandfather, was born in Cape Town in March 1815. Pieter married Sophia, who gave birth to the first of their three sons: Johan, Williem and Michiel.

All these names, I was getting confused, so flicked through a few pages and found the Family Tree.

It then became clearer and easier to follow. At first glance, there was a predominance of males on the van Vuuren side of the tree, with Jessica being the only female to be born a van Vuuren.

From Catherine's Vuuren Family Tree

- **Pieter van Vuuren** (1750-1810, born in Sas Van Gent, Zeeland, Netherlands
- **Dirk van Vuuren** (1781-1843.) married Wilhelmina Mijburgh
- **Pieter van Vuuren** (1815-1869.) married Sophia de Kock

- Johann van Vuuren (1840-1918.) married Elisabeth du Peez
- Brother: Michiel van Vuuren (1844-1870.
- Brother: Williem van Vuuren (b. 1846-1871.
- Wilhelm van Vuuren (b. 1882-1944.) married Elsie Meyer
- Joseph van Vuuren (b. 1915- 2002.) married Doris de Klerk
- Scott van Vuuren (b. 1948- 2003) married Janet Smith
- Sister: Catherine van Niekerk (1944- born Catherine van Vuuren.
- Jessica van Vuuren (b. 1986-
- Brother: Connor van Vuuren (b. 1990-

Having studied the van Vuuren side of the tree, I pushed on to the next chapter.

"Pieter van Vuuren became very prominent in the early formation of the Cape and at one stage became the Mayor of Cape Town, President of the Burgher Senate and member of the Legislative Council.
The family continued to prosper on the farm, Oranjeplassie. Johann was the hard worker and eventually took over the running of the farm, but his brothers had not inherited either their father's hardworking attitude or good nature. Williem and Michiel were both heavy drinkers and known for their violent, uncontrollable tempers and abusive behaviour towards their labourers and slaves, even to their wives on occasions.

Barely one year after their father's death, both their wives were mysteriously and brutally murdered. They hung two indigenous men for the crimes, however most believed the real culprits were closer to home, but the law was unwilling to challenge such men of wealth and power.

Despite the wealth and gaiety, the hosting of dinners, dances and hunting parties, it could not have been said that the van Vuuren's were a happy family!

I was now engrossed; the story was becoming interesting. No longer a list of names and dates, it was now painting a picture of murders and intrigues. Leaving me wanting to find out more; those two sons of Pieter's sounded like a right pair of bastards.

The van Vuuren's, however, progressively expanded their assets, as had been their policy since they arrived on this land full of promise and rich resources. Johann continued to expand their business interests until they owned the largest part of Table Valley. Two hundred and thirteen-morgen was acquired in the eighteenth century. Their primary income came from the sale of vegetables, fruit, and slaves.

They entertained on an extravagant scale, and dignitaries from far and wide would flock to their parties and lavish balls. Johann now lived in a fine mansion with his wife Elisabeth; the Cape Dutch architecturally built home featured one large gable above the front door which boasted the Family's Coat of Arms and the date of construction. The family were known for their opulence, which included their own in-house orchestra of thirty flute players in uniform who performed from the bandstand in the amphitheatre of the biggest garden.

The magnificent Oranjeplassie mansion was unique in the area, in that it was a double storey with wood-floor balcony in six columns. Inside, the rooms were cool with large windows, superb furnishings, an antique collector's paradise. Seven steps led from the paved pathway to the stoep, or veranda, the entrance to the house, tier after tier of terraced fields with stonework fronts stretched towards the mountain. It drew on the features reminiscent of Dutch townhouses, especially those found in Amsterdam; intricate, layered and complex defined by the grandiose rounded gables, the thatched roofs, and whitewashed walls. In front of the house was a fishpond surrounded by a cobbled courtyard, two slave bells hung suspended between two of the pillars.

These were rung at set hours, or in the case of an emergency or on sale days, when a flag would be hoisted. It was the signal for ship's officers, burghers, and children to proceed to the estate where they would meander through the spacious gardens, filling their baskets with fruit and vegetables, which would be weighed and paid for in the cobbled yard by the old oak tree. The exotic flowers adding colour to the occasion and the shady walks, making it a pleasurable day out for all.

The demise of Oranjeplassie started in 1857 when the Purchase Act enabled the Municipality to buy over twelve-morgen, on which to construct water reservoirs. Five years later, they released further portions of the estate and the municipality, who had also gained rights to seize the many springs on the estate; without water, the farm would struggle to survive.

The municipal land grabs and disputes over water; I was getting bored and tired of reading the book.

So, they owned a fruit farm that had a few problems: big deal! I would rather read the John Grisham novel that I had found earlier but knew that either mother or my sister would quiz me on the memoir later, so reluctantly pushed on…… my interest piqued again as I read the next chapter and learned about the diamonds.

With the farmland shrinking and yielding less profit, Johann van Vuuren knew that they would have to look further afield if they were to sustain the lifestyle to which the family had become accustomed. In 1867, news circulated that diamonds had been found along the banks of the Orange River in Hopetown. Without hesitation, Johann commissioned the building of fifteen ox-wagons; only the best for the van Vuuren's, built from hardy yellowwood, which was abundant in the Cape. They, too, would join the diamond rush to the Kimberleys. He sold off the remaining farmland; the van Vuuren family would set off on a new adventure.

His two brothers were not accustomed to hard work and had no desire to get their hands dirty. They declined the offer of going with Johann, so stayed and eked out a living doing whatever they could to maintain their drinking habits.

The wagons were finally built, and it was time for the family to begin their trek to the interior. The sturdy four-wheeled wagons started the long and dangerous journey, each pulled by twelve oxen and escorted by Johann's employees and several of their slaves.

It was a colourful scene as the train slowly departed from Oranjeplassie; sixty souls in total, men, women, children, and slaves. The men were excited and optimistic, whilst Elisabeth and the other women were less so. Despite showing determination and courage, they knew the trek would rupture their lives and those of their children and servants. They were aware of the dangers that might come from the chiefs of the indigenous tribes, who would be alarmed by the white men coming onto their lands by the hundreds and might become hostile.

They packed all their worldly possessions into the painted wagons, and they set out into uncharted territories. The men dressed in traditional short coats buttoned from top to bottom, hats, and leather thong shoes. The women in their flashy clothing with feathers, braiding and colorful stitching; it was a sight to behold.

The oxen struggled to move the overweighted wagons ladened with household goods, clothes, bedding, furniture, agricultural implements, fruit trees, and weapons. There were those wagons which would become mobile homes with canvas covers over the body of them. Johann was determined and promised that they could soon replicate the lavish lifestyle which they had enjoyed in Oranjeplassie, but first, they must survive the treacherous journey to Hopetown.

Once under way, those who were not walking had to cope with the uncomfortable feeling of the irregular thuds from the heavy and rough roads as the wagons rolled along the dirt tracks, whilst those on foot marched to the sound of a muffled drum being struck softly as they made their slow progress. The symphony of creaks, squeaks, and groans from the tortured wood of the wagon and the yoke and leather harnesses as they navigated potholes or turns could be heard by the venturers. Also, the clatter of the wooden wheels; the whish and thwack, as the driver used his crop or the sharp crack of the whip as he goaded the oxen forward.

The magnificent oxen, with their thick heavy breathing, getting louder as they tired and punctuated by sudden loud gusts through their open mouths and flapping lips; the steam hissing through nostrils, gusting forth on chilly mornings would pull these ox wagons, now adopted as an Afrikaans cultural symbol, they could carry up to seven tons and could navigate themselves over rocks and dongas; they were essential for any journeys across Africa in the eighteenth-and nineteenth centuries.

"*Goeiemore almal. Daar kom baie reen. Ek kan the volke sien. Die waens sal 'n laer vorm. Due kuddeseuns sal vir the osse sorg. Die kos sal uit die kombuiswa uitgerek word en sal bestaan uit pap en vleis. Ons sal vir 'n rukkie hier campeer om die stygende rivier te vermy".*

What on earth did that all mean?

I guess it was written in Afrikaans, but as I had never been to Africa in my life, it read more like "double Dutch".

I called mother, who managed to translate it for me.

Her version of the script was -

"The day had started beautiful; soon, however, this changed. Van Vuuren could not take the chance of being trapped in areas with the banks of the river bursting. This was the ideal place to camp for a few days."

"Thanks mum." She returned to the kitchen, and me to the book.

Van Vuuren's address was accepted with glee. Everyone had been getting more tired as each day progressed. Because of the clouds predicting heavy rains, the wagons would now form a laager. The herd boys would take care of the oxen, and the hearty meal of pap en vleis (stiff porridge and meat) would be available from the kitchen wagon. They would camp for a while to avoid the predicted rising of the river.

The wagons were being set in a laager, mainly for protection from any indigenous conflict in the area. As the moon turned the leaves into a patchwork of colour, scorching yellows, lava reds, and burnished browns, a huffing wind arose, stirring the canvas flaps on the wagons. The wind soon whipped up into a frenzy, its shrieking an omen of the carnage to follow. A tinkling sound came as the first pearls of rain dropped and soon the sound intensified, the winter sky bedarkened and weeping. Then the awaited deluge teemed down, flooding the rivers, drowning the veld as the floodgates in the sky opened.

The ferocity put all in physical danger as wagons were being blown, rolling from side to side. Children were crying, women showing their strength comforting all those around; the herd boys took shelter under the wagons, huddled together, only their white teeth glistening under the dark skies, as they comforted each other. Finally, on the eighth day, the sun burst through the sky. It brought with it a breath of fresh air, and they opened the wagons to dry out. A few days later, with the oxen rested, it was time to move on.

Day by day, the trekkers slowly advanced their wagon train into the interior and eventually the beasts of burden had delivered the van Vuuren's to Hopetown. The eight-hundred-mile journey had taken them over six months, but they had all arrived safely and been unmolested by any of the tribes along the way.

Being one of the first groups to arrive, Johann staked his claim to a large prime plot by the side of the Orange River, where the stone had been found.

As the news of the discovery spread, small parties of prospectors who had rushed to the area hoping to find similar stones soon surrounded them. Some of their neighbours were friendly, but others were less savoury. Wisely, Johann and his staff had come well-armed and ready to fight for what was theirs should it become necessary.

And so started the story of the van Vuuren's Diamond Mine.

"Lunchtime," called mother.

I reluctantly put in a marker, closed the book, and went through to the kitchen.

"Did you know we once owned a diamond mine in South Africa?" I asked Jess as we sat down at the table.

"No," she replied, as she took a bite of her bread roll.

"Surely you do. It's all in the book," I stated.

"Oh, the book," she sheepishly replied.

"Yes, the book, 'Flight to the New World.' You have actually read it, haven't you?"

"Not as such," she confessed. "I only flicked through the first few pages."

"Well! and you have the cheek to tell me what I should be reading."

"Ok brother, guilty as charged, but I have been meaning to. It's just that some of us have work to do. Anyway, what happened to the mine?"

"I'll let you know when I've finished, unless you intend to read it next?" I sarcastically enquired.

"No that's ok. I'll wait for your summarised version," she replied.

At this point mother intervened; unlike Jess, she had read the book.

"Apparently, there was a Diamond Mine and a family fortune that was stolen from the van Vuuren's."

"Continue reading Connor, I would be interested in your thoughts. I know that your father and his sister were both convinced that the South African Government robbed us. Not that there's anything that we could do about it now."

On that note, I bolted down the last of my lunch and returned to the book.

The first few months were hard and with little reward, as they slept under canvas while they built the first crudely erected huts for the workers. The property soon became a camp with a ring of shacks, huts and shelters constructed of any material that would keep off the rain or the scorching heat of the day. The van Vuuren's however, built for themselves a simple early Cape Dutch, thatched roof, and whitewashed farmhouse. This would serve as a temporary home as they continued to sift through the adjacent stream.

At this stage, they knew van Vuuren throughout the mining town as Lord Kimberley, as the dig became larger and larger. Drilling probe holes in the ground were being mapped, so the size of the hole was being enlarged bit by bit for economic reasons. To van Vuuren's surprise, one servant working for a party of diggers found diamonds in the most unexpected area. The temporary home which housed Lord Kimberley and his family was soon to be dismantled when diamonds were found in the mud-brick walls. The size of the hole was now increased and became colossal.

After six months of toiling, they had accumulated a small stash of smooth pebbles from the water, and this was the start of their mines. They were sufficient in number and size to inspire them to continue, now convinced that their stake would yield more riches.

After twelve months, they had accumulated enough to build a permanent home. They would set their own blueprint and, true to Van Vuuren style, this house would be the envy of the town. Soon, the foundations were laid. This Cape Dutch building would be the product of the Afrikaner Cape Colony established by the Dutch East India Company. It would exude tranquillity with its uneven, lime-washed walls. The softness and unevenness of the walls would be particularly striking under the strong African sun. The elaborately gabled house a clear indication of the hand of the mason who constructed it in the curves and flows of the gable form. Van Vuuren wanted grandeur and beauty of this house to go beyond the domain of the wealthy, to go beyond the aspirations of culture and its commissioners. He wanted this to represent the person whom he had become.

At the same time that van Vuuren was building and progressing, most of the neighbours had packed up their camps and left empty-handed, allowing van Vuuren to expand their mining area, slowly buying out the other smaller mines.

Three years later, the van Vuuren Mining Company was the largest in the region and the "blink klippe" (bright stones) continued to be found in these river diggings.

In 1875, an 81.5 carat diamond known as the 'Star of Hopetown' was discovered and the family fortune established.

The Star of Hopetown was never to be sold and would remain in the family forever. They had taken a common clear rock, polished it to a shine, restricted supply, made it a part of finding a lifelong lover and raised the prices. They found that there was nothing like falling for crude commercial manipulations to say, "I love you."

Wow! A fortune. So where did it go for God's sake?

The discoveries of the last chapter mesmerized me and calculated at today's prices, we should all be millionaires, not living on a penniless farm.

I turned the page to the next chapter but could not stop myself from flicking back to the previous one and re-reading about the mine.

Who would have believed that the news that a fourteen-year-old son of a poor Boer farmer, finding a shiny pebble, had led to the stampede of European settlers, mainly Dutch, selling up their small farms and heading inland to Hopetown; ultimately the creation of the van Vuuren fortune; but where was it now?

Impatient to find the answer, I started scanning through the next few chapters. I was also curious to find out whatever became of Johann's no-good brothers.

Johann was doing very well in the mining industry. Now well established, he was also looking at extending his investments, and being concerned for his two brothers, found a chance to make amends.

The Norman Hotel in Graaff-Reinet was completed in about 1800 and was originally the seat of Government for many years. It had gone through several structural changes during its lifetime, the latest owner having made plenty of alterations. Unfortunately, it then deteriorated, and Johann decided that this was his opportunity to not only buy this piece of property as his new investment, he would also engage the services of his two brothers to run the hotel. Michiel van Vuuren was a smart young man, albeit that he liked the alcohol. It was a new start in life, and he became the Commissioner-General, a post in a town that was torn by political dissension, and which had been menaced by the Xhosa since 1795.

Over the years, he did well to quell the unrest. As the Commissioner General, he paid particular attention to the restoration of public buildings, which included the Norman Hotel. He also quelled the disturbances caused by the Xhosa, the detribalized Hottentots and to the Bushmen who were raiding the north-western parts of the district. In return, he tried to reconcile with the Bushmen and prevent their starving to death by arranging for game to be shot for them and periodically giving them cattle. This compromise for the Bushmen worked well, however, the relationship of the Xhosa would continue to deteriorate.

Johann felt he had done as much as he could and was happy with the way his two brothers were working and running the hotel. However, he was devastated when he later heard that Michiel had been killed in a skirmish between an English and Afrikaans faction in a bar fight and his brother Williem had died after contracting syphilis a year later.

I must confess to having mixed emotions when reading that section; glad to hear that the pair had got their just deserts, though upon reflection, I knew that none of us were perfect as my mind wandered back to Afghanistan.

I refocused my thoughts, turned to the next page and started reading the accounts of the two Boer Wars.

During this time, he had to contend with the effects of the first Boer War in 1880, which only lasted a few months and ended in March 1881. There were several accounts of how the Boers had the upper

hand over the British Empire forces and basically had sent them off with their tails between their legs.
In 1899, the Second Anglo Boer War was well under way.
There had been heavy losses on both sides. The Boers started well, their commandos moving quickly across the land, attacking the British supply lines where they inflicted heavy losses, but the British reinforcements just kept coming and coming; eventually the conflict ended. A victory to the British, although most observers described it as a no score draw.
Both sides had suffered severe losses and typhoid had swept across the country, taking thousands of lives. Many of those were women, children, and prisoners who had been housed in the makeshift concentration camps.

The accounts in the book sent shivers down my spine, and the comparisons to Afghanistan flashed through my mind. The untrained Boers being called to arms, the only requirements being that they were sixteen years old, owned a rifle and a horse.

And for what? So that the Brits could continue to plunder Africa for its untapped resources; and on this occasion it was the gold and diamonds.

Johann had been too old to be called up to fight, but his only son, Wilhelm, and three of his best men were, so they rode off to war. Sadly Wilhelm was the only one to return.
After the war, he and his father had kept the rights to his mines.

The light was fading, and my eyes were getting tired.

The last chapter and the vivid descriptions of death and destruction had reduced me to tears; man's inhumanity to man had not changed over the last hundred years.

I had read enough for today, so wiped my eyes and closed the book; the last few chapters could wait until tomorrow.

"Connor, dinner's ready," a voice from the kitchen called me in.

I joined the others at the table, although I had no great appetite, and toyed with my food.

"What's up? You've hardly touched your dinner," Jess asked.

"Nothing really, it's just that Aunt paints a very sad picture of South Africa. It's a bit more graphic than I had expected."

"So, what about the fortune?" she eagerly asked.

"You'll have to wait until tomorrow, not quite got to that part yet. If you'll all excuse me, I need an early night. All this reading has given me a headache." I stood and left my half-eaten plate of food. I knew I would struggle to sleep and feared that the nightmares might return, so pressed Jess for some sleeping pills. She reluctantly succumbed, and I got a little sleep until awoken by the light of dawn.

As soon as I finished breakfast, I took the book out onto the deck and opened it up again: Chapter 6; only a few more to go.

"The Anglo Boer War was over, life returned to normal, and under Wilhelm's management, the van Vuuren Mine Company continued to prosper, being the largest in the region.

Johann, now in the twilight of his years, lived in the magnificent marble-built mansion aptly named the 'Star of Hope' with Wilhelm and all the family.

When your name is on a million lips, it is your world, and that amount of space is necessary. The mansion was a status symbol, befitting the wealthiest man in the state, but again, it brought little happiness; Wilhelm and Elise choosing to set up a home of their own several miles away.

In 1914, Wilhelm was off to war again, this time ironically fighting with the British against the Germans. During World War I, the mines were closed and several of the van Vuuren's Kimberley mines were never to re-open; however worse was yet to come.

Wilhelm had enlisted in the South African Expeditionary Forces as a Private in the 7th Infantry regiment. He had only served for two months before he was wounded in action, having been shot through the chest at Salaita Hill, East Africa and was subsequently invalided and sent back to Cape Town. It was just in time for the birth of Joseph van Vuuren, who Elise delivered to him in 1915.

In 1918 came the outbreak of the Great Flu.

Wilhelm and Elise both contracted the Spanish Flu and were down and unconscious in bed because of the fever.

Elise was the first to regain her consciousness and found little Joseph, the three-year-old toddler at her side. He had been cared for by the housekeeper and unaffected by the epidemic.

When Wilhelm eventually regained consciousness, he was met with the tragic news that the 'Star of Hope' had gone up in flames.

His elderly father, Johann van Vuuren, had perished in the blaze along with two of the servants. It had been burned to the ground, and the authorities believed it to have been an arson attack.

This news destroyed Wilhelm, as if the years of warfare were not enough to leave him shell-shocked; losing his father nearly pushed him over the edge. Unable to work, he employed more managers and rarely visited the mines; all enthusiasm had gone, and he withdrew from society a broken man.

For Joseph, it was a different story; The van Vuuren's had survived the Great Flu, and despite both parents being down cast, Joseph always remained full of life and happiness, even in the driest and most difficult times.

He grew up and was doing well in high school when the big drought broke out. Cracks grew deep in the barren, parched soil. The river became a trickle. After so many months of no rain, it was barely a stream moving listlessly over the stones it usually disregarded in its swift passage to the Indian Ocean. Hence, Joseph interrupted his school career, as they needed him to help his family in the mines.

His mother called him her Karoo blometjie, after the tiny Karoo blooms whose green leaves always looked fresh, even in the driest and most difficult times, albeit he had the fresh complexion, blue eyes, and brown hair of his father. He was the chestnut and the acorn, the seed of everything good to come. He was their brown-haired boy.

The van Vuuren family survived thanks to the mercies of family and neighbours. Nevertheless, they lost almost everything on their farming property, which they had before the drought.

Joseph spent every minute in the mines, and by the age of eighteen, he knew as much about mining as any of the managers, and soon assumed his father's role as head of the company. He had matriculated at Hopetown High School in 1934 as one of the top matriculants of the former Union of South Africa. He then studied at Stellenbosch and would eventually become known as "The Miner".

He had also become a competent flyer, regularly taking his small plane between their various mines around Hopetown and Cape Town, where he had moved their offices as the company continued to expand. The family mansion was rebuilt, but not on the original site in Hopetown, now in the quiet leafy suburbs of Cape Town.

Then the writing style changed, as Aunty described the events of the second world war in Europe, drawing me back into the sadness and emotions of yet another war.

"Joseph had not forgotten their families' Dutch origins and was quick to enlist in the RAF as a fighter pilot; he then spent the next few years in England leaving his wife Doris to run the company. Joseph, or Joe as his fellow pilots had taken to calling him, had spent most of the war flying Spitfires and protecting the British coastline from the German bombers. Despite being shot down on two occasions, he was one of the lucky ones to survive the battle of the skies. The only saving grace was that he had never met the enemy face-to-face. Unlike his father, Wilhelm had done in the trenches of East Africa, which ultimately drove him crazy.

After the war, life in South Africa continued as before, but things were about to change.

In 1948, Doris gave birth to Scott van Vuuren. It was the same year as Jan Christiaan Smuts lost the General Election to Daniel Malan of the National Party, who then enforced a policy of segregation. This policy resulted in sanctions from most countries in the Western World and was not good for the van Vuuren Mining Company.

Scott grew up in a segregated society between the Europeans and the Bantu people. Political unrest and the constant threats of violence, made for a nervous existence, so when his wife gave birth to Jessica in 1986, he emigrated to Australia, along with his sister Catherine and her family.

Joe refused to budge; South Africa was where he was born, and it was where he would spend his last days.

On the 7th of November 1986, the van Vuuren family made another epic journey, this time not in ox-drawn wagons but first class aboard a South African Airways flight to Australia.

Apartheid continued in South Africa until the nineteen-nineties, when President FW de Klerk released Nelson Mandela from prison, Mandela subsequently became President and appointed de Klerk as his deputy.

As the African National Congress gained control of the country, it became increasingly difficult for European owned business to survive, but Joe dug his heels in and was determined to continue running his company.

In 2005, there was a phone call from one of his managers, informing Scott that his father had died. It was no surprise to the family; Joe was just short of his ninetieth birthday and had smoked like a chimney all his life.

Scott and Catherine returned to Cape Town for the funeral and travelled to Graaff-Reinet, where the ceremony would be held. They chose this church as it was special to the family; not only had Johann had his funeral ceremony here, but in his early years had donated the piece of land and six windows for the Dutch Reformed missionary church to be built.

Like his father before him, they honoured Joseph for the life that he had. The many years when he was involved in the mining industry and the years that he spent as a fighter pilot. The family was still held in high esteem in the district which afforded Scott and Catherine the best of hospitality.

When they returned to Cape Town to attend to the business matters about the mine, they were informed that it had been taken over by the African National Congress and would be nationalized under the new government.

The robbing bastards! I stormed into the kitchen and confronted mother, who was busy preparing dinner.

"Surely this can't be right?"

"Right or not, it is what happened. There was to be no inheritance. The South African Government took the lot. Your father and his sister even spent a fortune on solicitors, only to be informed that there was nothing to be done. Everything is gone, Connor, including the 'Star of Hopetown' diamond."

My heart sank. This cannot be right. Is there no justice in this world? I dropped the book onto the kitchen table. There were a few pages still to go, although now I had lost the desire to finish them, and slumped into a chair.

Mother wiped her hands and sat beside me.

"The hours that your father spent contacting Joseph's friends and associates to find a way around it. But with no desire to return to South Africa, we were met with one brick wall after another; there was no way of bypassing the bureaucracy and selling off what was ours by right. Anyway, it's all in the past now, unless you have some kind of magic wand."

"Sadly not," I replied, then picked up the book and went to my room.

I lay on my bed. Dinner would not be ready for an hour, so clutching the manuscript to my chest, I tried to close my eyes. The injustice of it all! I couldn't wait for Jess to return. Surely there must be something that we could do.

But what?

After dinner, I sat out on the deck with Jess and gave her a shortened version of Aunt Cath's story.

"Is she still alive?" I asked.

"As far as I know, why?"

"I want to know more about her last visit to Cape Town with father, and who she talked to."

"That was over fifteen years ago when grandpa died, and it has got to be at least twenty years since either of us saw her, anyway mum thinks she has gone gaga since then."

"Well, gaga or not, she'll still know more about South Africa than we do," I insisted.

"What's this all about, brother?" she suspiciously asked.

"I was just asking." I nonchalantly replied.

She leaned forward and quietly asked, "Do you have a plan?"

"I might. Only time will tell. Let's go for a walk."

***

Chapter 4

It was a quiet morning. Patrick had not planned on moving any cattle, so after breakfast, Jess offered to take me out for a ride. Mother packed a coffee flask and made a few sandwiches. We saddled our mounts and set off towards the mountains.

After an hour's ride, my bum was sore, so we found a sheltered spot in the shade by a billabong, watered the horses and settled for a mug of coffee.

Jess fetched a notepad from her saddlebag, and we started planning.

"So, master criminal, how are we going to steal back what is ours?" she asked in a slightly belittling fashion.

"I'm no master crim, but I've been involved in enough operations to know that planning is the key to success. Now, are you going to take this seriously or not?"

"Sorry brother. Do you really think that we can do it?"

"We have two choices, either to spend the rest of our lives bemoaning our luck or getting our arses into gear and giving it our best shot. Which is it to be?"

"Ok, let's do it," and she took out a pencil to make notes.

I cast my mind back to my days in Special Ops; the briefing room and the Commanding Officer outlining the operations. I now had to put myself in his shoes. This was to be my baby; I was now the one in charge and started with the sub-headings.

Aims & objectives, personnel, financing, transport, passports, and firearms should it become necessary; all would be essential to our success.

"That sounds an impressive list Connor, though I don't like the thoughts of using guns."

"Hopefully they will never become needed, but if we end up committing a robbery in South Africa and hope to get out alive, it'll be no cakewalk." I tried to reassure her, without making it sound like a suicide mission.

"Ok, where shall we start, aims and objectives or personnel?" she asked and prepared to write.

"The aims and objectives: To go to Cape Town, find out who has our diamonds, and reclaim them by any means; fair or foul." I took a swallow of coffee and continued. "Information is key, so firstly we need to visit Aunt Catherine and find out exactly how much she knows. After that we'll need to recruit a team to help us carry out this mission."

"A team! who do you think you are, Tom Cruise? Where the hell do we find a gang of international robbers? No, don't tell me; advertise on the internet." My sister never missed an opportunity to make fun of her younger brother.

"Not exactly," I calmly replied. "I know several ex-special forces who'd run the risk, on the chance of making a fortune: you can leave the personnel to me."

"Ok you're the expert, so what about finances, I guess these friends of yours would want to be paid, then there is the problem of air tickets, where are we going to find the money, it's a bloody long walk to Africa!"

"You are right Jess, there are loads of logistical problems to sort out, let's take one step at a time; we need to visit Aunty in Perth."

We finished our picnic, remounted, and took a slow ride back to the farm.

The four of us sat around the table. Mother had just finished serving lunch when Jess had the irresistible urge to make a public announcement.

"Connor and I are going to Cape Town," she blurted out.

"Sorry, you're going where?" asked mother.

"We're going to South Africa; we need to find out what happened to our diamonds. Someone has them and we want them back; it's just not fair!" she stated.

"Your dad went through all this when he was alive. The lawyers could get nowhere, so how do you think that the pair of you will?"

I then explained to mother and Patrick that we were putting together a plan, we could no longer sit back knowing there was a fortune belonging to us, and we had been guilty of accepting no for an answer, instead of fighting for what is ours.

"We only have one slight problem at the moment: the question of financing our little adventure. I was rather hoping that you and Patrick might help out?" I tentatively asked, but did not expect a positive response.

"We would if we could, but we are up to our necks in bank loans as it is." After mother's last comment, there was a protracted, uncomfortable silence.

"I'd really like to help," offered Patrick, "but your mother's right, we've not shown a profit for three years, and it's not looking too good this year either."

"What about Aunt Catherine.? She married well. The van Niekerk's are worth a bit. She might help," suggested mother. "Her husband sold their farm before they emigrated. They lost a bit on the sale, but still got enough money out of the country to set themselves up nicely in Western Australia."

That was not a bad idea, however we still had to get to Perth, and I doubted that Jess's old car could stand the journey. Renting a Ute would be a better option. It would be better still if I could borrow a truck from Patrick. We avoided the embarrassment of me asking, as he was the first to offer the use of his Toyota, so long as we returned it by the following week.

The next morning, Jess and I set off on the 40-hour journey. It would be longer if we made any overnight stops, so we initially planned to share the driving and press on through the nights, stopping only for petrol or the call of nature.

Mother had packed a hamper of provisions, along with two gallons of drinking water, and Patrick handed us an envelope with a thousand dollars, to cover fuel and emergencies. We thanked them both and set off on the first step of our adventure.

We split the first 16-hours into two-hour shifts as we made our way south. The sat-nav informed us we still had another 24-hours to go, travelling west towards the Indian Ocean. It was now 10pm; we were both fatigued and bored with the monotony of driving, so the original plans went out of the window, and we spent the next eight hours sleeping in a motel.

In the morning, we hurriedly ate the all-inclusive breakfast, filled the Ute at the Servo, and excitedly went on our way. This was the longest section of our journey, and seemed to go on forever, as we crossed the seemingly endless red landscape of the Nullarbor Plane. The only relief was when the Eyre Highway took us along the coastal road, where we could see the spectacular Great Australian Bite.

Once again, we succumbed to our tired eyes, so made another stop. This time in the small town of Balladonia; knowing that it would only leave us another 500km to drive the next day.

We arrived on the outskirts of Perth in the afternoon and followed the sat-nav to the address that mother had written for us.

The van Niekerk's lived in a plush mansion overlooking the Swan River.

I'm no estate agent, but I guess that all the homes along their avenue would be valued over 5 million.

I carefully drove up the palm lined gravelled driveway and parked Patrick's dirty looking Ute between the pristine Bentley and Ferrari that stood outside their garage. We then walked across the manicured lawns to the main entrance. Jess gave me a quick brush down with her hand and straightened my collar, pulled her shoulders back, and boldly rang the doorbell.

We stood there and waited apprehensively. There was no reply, so Jess pressed again. On the second attempt, a middle-aged woman in a housecoat opened the door. I was about to step forward to greet her with an embrace, then stopped in my tracks, as I realised it was not Aunt Catherine, but their housekeeper.

"May I help you?" she politely asked.

"Is Aunty Catherine in? I'm her niece and this is my brother; we're visiting from Queensland."

The woman eyed us suspiciously before asking us to wait, whilst she found out if the van Niekerk's were at home.

"At home? My, we are in a posh neighbourhood," I whispered to Jess with a grin once the woman's back was turned.

A minute later and she returned.

"They are in the conservatory, please come through," and she led us through the magnificently furnished building; the pair of us really felt like the poor relatives.

Catherine's husband, Daniel van Niekerk, was a large jovial man in his mid-seventies, who had never lost his broad Afrikaans accent. Since arriving in Australia, he had invested in property development; it was the boom years in Perth and after thirty-five years, he had amassed a small fortune.

Daniel lifted his hefty frame from the armchair and welcomed us both with a smile and a warm handshake.

In contrast, Aunt Catherine was a small, delicate creature. Smartly dressed and in full make-up, despite it being the middle of the afternoon. Her welcoming embrace was awkward, which was not surprising, as we had not met for many years.

"Well, how the pair of you have grown, I would hardly have recognised either of you." Spoken softly, but I could see what she was thinking, there was an element of distrust in her voice; Why had we suddenly appeared on their doorstep?

"Drinks? Tea, coffee, or would you like a cold one?" offered Daniel.

"Coffees would be good," Jess replied, answering for the pair of us.

"Don't just stand there, come and sit down," invited Aunty, then called the housekeeper. "Could you fetch us a pot of coffee, please?"

"So, how's life treating you? Are you still living on the farm in Burgville?" Daniel enquired.

"Yes, still herding cattle," replied Jess with a smile and added, "mother and Patrick send their regards."

"What about you," he asked me, "still in the army?"

I was tempted to lie and say yes but knew that Jess would blow me out if I did, so told them the full story, omitting the part about my nightmares.

My ten years in the SAS, my tours in Afghanistan, retiring from the service, and my struggle to come to terms with civilian life. My account interrupted only by Jess proudly interjecting to mention my citations for bravery.

"So what now, are you going to be a farmer or are you looking for another line of work; is that what you are here for?" asked Daniel, who had listened patiently and with interest.

"Not really, we are here about Aunty Catherine's book," I replied and cast a smile in her direction.

"My book," she beamed, "have you read my book?"

"Yes Aunt, it's a fascinating account of our family history; I was glued to it for days. Particularly the part about the diamonds, was that all true, or did you use a bit of poetic licence?"

"Sadly, all true. Your father and I did all that we could to reclaim our family fortunes, but we got nowhere; what is gone is gone." Her sad eyes reflected her resignation.

"Well, why we are here is because we think that as a family we caved in too easily. If the diamonds are still there, we intend to get them back!" Jess urged.

"And how in God's name do you intend to do that?" asked Daniel with a grin, as though he were talking to two silly little children.

"By negotiation if we can, by force if we can't." I insisted.

Daniel leant forward in his chair. Now he was all ears and taking us more seriously.

"Tell me more Connor."

I outlined my experiences working in Special Ops, the personnel and expertise that were at my disposal; many of my colleagues were now out of the services and would be keen to become involved in such an operation, if the rewards were there. I reassured him that recruitment would not be a problem.

"So, why have you come to me with your outlandish ideas. Sure, I'd like to see you get what you can from those thieving bastards, but where do I fit in to your plans? I'm an elderly businessperson, not a young villain."

It was a fair question that deserved an honest answer, so I got straight to the point.

"Money, I need your money. Without a financial backer, I can't get this plan off the ground. You're a businessperson Daniel, so see this as an investment opportunity."

He pondered my last statement and poured himself a scotch.

"If, and I only mean if." He paused, "If I were to invest there are two obvious questions, one how much would you need and secondly, what would my return be on such a gamble; assuming of course that you were successful?"

My confidence rose now that I had his attention, and I pitched my case before I outlined the initial costs.

First, I would need to go back to Brisbane and recruit my team, which would comprise of Jess and I, plus three others. The three that I had in mind were my old mate, Alex. He was an expert electrician and a brilliant all-round techie; his pal Jason, a top man in firearms and explosives; then possibly Charlie from the farm, if Patrick could spare him. Charlie was not a big man, but as strong as an ox and handy in a fight; a good man to have covering your back.

A five Grand retainer each should hold their interest before we put any plan into action.

Whilst in Brisbane, I would need to speak with Major Simpson, who had been in Military Intelligence most of his service and had endless contacts all around the globe, including South Africa; I might need to pay him a sweetener for his information.

Jess, Alex, and I would fly out to Cape Town to reconnoitre and attempt a diplomatic solution. If we failed, we would start putting a plan together before returning to Australia, assuming that the Star of Hopetown was still to be found.

The diamond is priceless. It would fetch millions on the open market. Aunt Catherine, Jess and I are the last in the van Vuuren's line, so I suggested a three-way split.

Daniel had listened attentively; it obviously impressed him with our enthusiasm, however, clearly not a man to make rash decisions.

"We'll talk again in the morning; I'll need the night to sleep on it." He then offered to take his poor relatives to dinner at an expensive restaurant by the river.

Over the meal, we quizzed Catherine about her book, which she happily expounded upon, obviously proud of her research and writings.

Daniel was a cheerful host. He talked endlessly on every subject, though never once mentioning my proposals. By the time we returned to the mansion and settled in the guest rooms, I had convinced myself that it would be a nonstarter; I despondently tried to sleep, in the belief that our three-day drive had been a total waste of time.

But after breakfast the next day, he slid a thick brown envelope across the table.

"Fifty Grand, it should be enough to float your boat until you get back from Cape Town. Make Perth your first stop on your return. I like to be kept informed; we'll talk money again then." Daniel then added, "It might provide enough material for your Aunt to write a sequel to her book."

A feeling of relief, delight, and amusement as I watched the open-mouthed Jess choke on her coffee.

We keenly shook him by the hand; all I had to do now was to put my words into actions and turn our dreams into reality.

***

Chapter 5

The Sat-Nav had predicted a forty-five-hour return to Brisbane, if we drove continuously through the night; this time we had no such ambitious ideas, so Jess rang a few motels while I drove; she then rang home.

She assured Patrick that we were on our way back, but that we needed to stop off in Brisbane for a night. We would get the Ute back as soon as possible, and should he need wheels in the meantime, the Beetle's keys were hanging up in the kitchen.

"Patrick didn't sound too impressed with that. So, when do you think we'll be home, brother?" she asked when she'd finished her call.

"I need to speak to Alex and his mate Jason to sell the idea. Then I really must speak to Major Simpson. He's a mine of information; I'm hoping that he will put us in touch with the right people in Cape Town."

"What do you mean by the *'Right People'*, right in what way?"

"Well, should we need firearms, we can't just pack them into our suitcases, we will need to know where we can get them, and also who we can trust."

Jess sat quietly, and I could see that her brain was racing, as the realisation was striking home; South Africa would not be a holiday trip, it was going to be business!

The drive across the Nullarbor was no more interesting than before, dirty, dusty, and a seemingly endless road; we were only happy when handing over the driving to the other.

The two overnight stops were more comfortable; thanks to Daniel we could now afford a better class of motel.

Three days of travelling and we arrived in Brisbane.

I had phoned ahead to Alex, who offered the sofa in the bedsit for us to bunk down on; I politely declined. We could afford a smart hotel in the city, and I insisted he stay overnight with us and see if Jason might like to join us.

"Love to. Where are you staying?" asked Alex.

"We have booked in at the Grand; shall we say dinner at seven o'clock?"

"The Grand! Have you just won the fuckin' lottery?" he asked in disbelief.

"Not quite, but I'll explain over dinner tonight. Make sure you get Jason to come. You may both be interested in what I have to say. Got to go, the traffic is building up, see you at seven," and ended the call.

Once we had parked up in the Grand Hotel, we showered and then headed for the shops; if I wanted to convince them to join our venture, then image would be everything; we both needed to look the part, not some comedy duo.

I chose a tailored dark grey suit, and a selection of shirts, when I say I, of course I mean under the supervision of my sister, who apparently knew what suited me better than I did.

As I stood in front of the mirror admiring myself, I had to admit that she was right, a total transformation from 'Bum' to 'businessman'.

That evening Jess and I waited in the Hotel bar for our guests, both in our smart new suits and crisp white shirts, looking as though we had just stepped out of a fashion magazine.

Ten minutes later, they stood at the door, looking rather lost. I waved and beckoned them over to the bar. Both had tried with their appearance, the handsome, athletic figure of Alex wearing jeans, blazer, and an open-necked pastel blue shirt, Jason in a jacket and mismatching pants, his short muscular frame, always looked good in uniform, but never in civvies, and his shirt had seen better days; it was clean but frayed at both the collar and cuffs.

Introductions and handshakes exchanged; I had not seen Jason since we left the service and was keen to find out what he had been doing for the last two years.

Alex offered to get the drinks in, I assured him that the drinks, meal, and accommodation were on me, then handed him a Myer's bag.

"What's all this? It's not my birthday," Alex asked as he peered into the bag.

"I know, they are replacements for the shirts that I borrowed when I left."

"Cheers Connor, who chose them, you or Jess? No, don't answer that, they are far too good to be of your choosing," he cheekily commented, then turned to Jess and gave her a peck on the cheek.

"Hilarious; another drink guys, or shall we go through to our table?"

The restaurant was busy, so I tipped the Maître de to find us a quiet table in the corner.

Jess chose the wine, although Jason preferred to stick with the beer, and we chatted idly for ten minutes before ordering our meals.

"Well Connor, quite a bloody transformation mate!! The last time I saw you was when you were arrested for that brawl in the nightclub. And in all honesty, I thought the Judge would send you down. It's not like it was the first time."

"Yes, I got lucky. Mike Simpson turned up and put in a friendly word for me, and I caught the Magistrate on a good day. Anyway, a lot has happened since then."

"Yes, Connor's world has change; he read a book!" Jess butted in.

Why does she always do that? She can never resist the opportunity of making another quip at my expense.

"I think that what Jessica is trying to say is that I discovered my grandfather owned a diamond mine in South Africa. When he died, the thieving government stole the fortune that should rightfully be ours."

"That sounds pretty rough, doesn't explain the new threads though, and splashing out the cash, so what gives?" pressed Alex.

"What gives is that we have a backer. We intend to go over there and reclaim our diamonds. We'll start by asking nicely, but if they don't want to play, a second visit may become necessary to extract what is ours."

"When you say extract, am I right in assuming that you mean by force?" asked Jason as his eyes lit up.

"It's what we all do well, so tonight is just about asking the pair of you a question. Are you interested in a share of our millions?"

They both sat there open-mouthed, then Alex burst out laughing.

"Well done Connor. Nice one mate, you nearly got me going there you bugger."

"Me too," added Jason, who was obviously disappointed. His face dropped like a child who'd just had his toys taken away, then asked, "So where's this menu; I'm starving."

Jess gave me a smile and picked up her bag from under the table.

"It's not a joke gentlemen, it is a serious proposition. Think about it overnight and we can talk again in the morning. In the meantime, take this gift, see it either as a retainer, or an inducement to keep your mouths shut, should you not wish to join us." She then handed them each an envelope. "There's five grand in each. Count it once you've left the table."

"Right lads, what do you want to eat?" and I summoned the waiter for the menus.

Over the meal, we spent much of the time reminiscing about the good old days, although our stories were exaggerated in the retelling; the three of us had enjoyed the comradeship that is forged in the heat of battle, we all carried the scars; both physical and psychological.

Alex had left the service as a qualified electrician and walked straight into a job with his uncle's building firm. He wasn't earning a fortune, but it was steady work.

Jason, like me, had no recognised qualifications. We were both skilled in the theatre of war, unfortunately our talents were not transferable to civilian life. He was fit and strong, so had no trouble in finding unskilled work as a labourer wherever he could find it.

By the time we left the table, I felt confident that they would join us. It would be a gamble, but none of us had anything to lose.

At breakfast the next morning, it was all smiles and handshakes.

Yes! They were both up for it.

We exchanged mobile numbers, and I promised to keep Jason updated.

Alex made a call to his uncle. He could not work for a month, as he might have to be out of the country on urgent business.

I then made a call to Major Mike Simpson.

"Good morning Sir, it's Connor van Vuuren."

"Morning Connor, what is it this time? I'm very busy, and don't have the time to come to court again," he replied with a sigh.

"No Sir, it's nothing like that. I'd like to invite you to lunch."

"Lunch? Sorry Connor, I'm not falling for that one. I told you last time there'll be no more handouts from me."

"No, you've got it wrong. I mean lunch at the Grand, my treat this time."

There was a pause at the other end of the line.

"Have you any idea how much it costs at the Grand?" Simpson quietly asked.

"Yes, I do. I'm staying there at the moment. You told me to pull my shit together, so I did. I promise you I'm not wasting your time. I need to pick your brains and I'm happy to pay for your expertise, and I don't just mean with a free meal."

There was another pause.

"Ok Connor, you've got me intrigued. I appear to have a space in my diary, so shall we say lunch at one o'clock."

I now felt the hardest part was over. At our last meeting we had not parted on good terms; fortunately, 'Mad Mike' Simpson, as they affectionately knew him amongst his men, was not a man to hold a grudge.

1.00pm. precisely, he entered the restaurant and the Maître de showed him to our table.

I stood to welcome him.

"You know Alex."

"Of course," and Mike held out his hand. "But who's this beautiful young lady? Surely she doesn't belong to either of you two ugly brutes."

"No Sir, she's mine by default. May I introduce you to my sister Jessica?"

'Mad Mike' was well known in the regiment; fifty years old, handsome with thick greying hair, immaculately dressed in a dark suit and wearing the regimental tie; a real ladies' man who could charm the birds out of the trees.

He had caused me to look again at my tomboy sister, now in her mid-thirties, her red hair normally tied back in a ponytail, now shining, and hanging loose upon her shoulders. Yes, Mike was right. She was a beautiful woman.

"A pleasure to meet you," and he politely took her hand and kissed it; what a bloody smoothy!

I had been unsure whether to approach Simpson alone, or with Jess and Alex. By the smile on his face, I was confident that I had made the right decision; he would take any opportunity to impress the ladies.

"So, Connor, how may I help you? Not that it appears you need much help; quite a change since our last encounter," he said as he looked me up and down approvingly.

"Shall we eat first, then talk business?" I asked as I beckoned the waiter.

"Why not do both? As I said earlier, I am very busy."

Between mouthfuls, Jess and I told of our lost fortune, to which the Major listened patiently, and without interruption. This was not through indifference, but because he was a man who always wanted to have received all the facts before passing comment.

By the time we got to the coffee, our tale had been told and our intentions made clear.

"That's quite some story and I don't doubt that most of it is true, but what do you want of me?" he asked.

"Well, at this moment, we would be going in blind. We don't know who to talk to, or where to get our hands on any equipment that we might need. You have contacts everywhere; I would be amazed if you didn't have any in Africa."

"I couldn't possibly admit to that now. I would need to know more, also what you have to offer."

He was a cool character, then again, so were most of the men who had worked in Special Ops.

"The 'Star of Hopetown' is priceless. It's the biggest stone to be found in Africa; on the open market we would be talking millions. Subject to what assistance you give us, I could cut you 10% as a finder's fee." I proudly stated.

"10% of nothing does not look too tempting," he raised his eyebrows and stared me in the face.

"Hardly anything. You'll be on a retainer as well, should it all go pear-shaped?" Jess cut in.

"Ok then, 10k and I'll make a few phone calls," he offered.

Jess retrieved an envelope from her bag and handed it to me, and I slid it across the table to Simpson.

"Ok Major, Ten Grand, we'll speak again tomorrow."

He looked at his watch, then stood up.

"I had best be off and start earning my money," he said with a smile. "It has been a pleasure to meet you Miss van Vuuren;" we shook hands, and he left.

"So, do you really think that this Mad Mike character can come up with the goods?" asked Jess.

"I do hope so. We're burning through Daniel's cash and haven't even bought our tickets to Cape Town yet."

"Don't worry you two, if Mad Mike says he'll do it he will. We've put our lives in his hands many times and he's never let us down." Alex reassured us.

We returned to our room, and we spent the rest of the day on Alex's laptop, researching the political situation in South Africa and flights to Cape Town.

Our dream was becoming a reality. All we needed was for the Major to come up with the goods. Without his help, we would have no chance.

The following morning, we had a call from Mike to arrange another meeting, this time at a café close to his office.

The four of us sat around a quiet table in the corner, away from any prying eyes, nervously awaiting Mike's disclosures; Jess poised with a pen and notepad.

"That won't be necessary," and he slid a buff envelope across the table, "Ok guys, I spent most of the night on the phone and eventually got hold of Kurt Muller, he worked for South African intelligence back in the nineties, now freelance and working for the Libyan Government. Kurt has spent the last six months in Johannesburg, trying to track down the billions that Gadhafi had stashed away down there, before his downfall. But like your diamonds, the cash seems to have vanished into thin air." He paused for a sip of coffee.

"That doesn't sound too promising," butted in Jess.

"Be patient, I haven't finished yet." He put down his coffee and continued.

"Kurt is pretty sure the cash is out of the country. Tomas Zimbala, the recently deposed President, skipped the country and now lives in exile in neighbouring Mozambique, along with a large stash of cash, hoping to finance his return to power."

"How does that help us?" asked Jess.

"Well, I mentioned the 'Star of Hopetown' to Kurt. He had heard of it, also that it was last seen in the possession of Tomas Zimbala before he fled the country."

"That makes sense, so how do we contact this Kurt Muller?" I keenly asked.

"It's all in the folder, including a recent photo of the man. I can arrange a meeting, but I must remind you that Kurt is freelance. I'm helping because I know you guys; he doesn't, so ten grand would not impress him; it might take a lot more than that."

"How much more?" asked Jess.

"He has a lot of hungry mouths to feed; I'd offer Fifty to start with and see what he says."

"How big is his family?" she naively asked.

"We're not talking children, I mean police, government officials and the like," he replied with a grin. "In Africa everyone wants a slice of the cake."

"It's sounding like a military operation. What about equipment?" asked Alex.

"Depends on whether you get Kurt on board, if you do, he'll get his hands on anything you need, but again, it won't come cheap," warned Mike, then reminded me that the file in the folder was not for export, once read it must be destroyed.

Despite his request, Jess continued to make notes until she felt we had all the information that we needed.

We thanked Mike and returned to the Hotel to rethink our plans. The Major's information had changed everything.

Perth would now be our next stop. Daniel would need to top up our coffers. This would not be a cheap venture; I just hoped that his pockets were deep enough.

Logistically, we needed to forget returning to Burgville, which would mean leaving Charlie out of the equation. It would be one less ticket and not deprive Patrick of another hand on the farm. It would not be difficult to have the Ute returned, a visit to the Backpacker

Hotel and I would easily find a willing volunteer who would do it for a few bucks.

I phoned Jason and told him to meet us at the hotel, pack a bag, and bring his passport. Jess then booked four seats on the next Brisbane to Perth flight.

Four hours later, we booked out of the Grand and boarded a taxi to the Airport.

***

Chapter 6

"How Much!" exclaimed Catherine in disbelief.

"Another hundred thousand," I tentatively replied. Having seen the look on her face, I thought I was in for a struggle to convince them. Daniel had not spoken. He just looked down at his feet, deep in concentration.

"Ok." He raised his head and looked me in the eye and continued, "That's no surprise. I know how everyone does business over there. When do you want it?"

"As soon as we have booked the fights," I replied with a sigh of relief.

He then wrote a series of numbers on a notepad, tore it off, and handed it to me.

"It's my old account in Cape Town. I'll wire the money across; it'll be there before you arrive. Any problems, ask to speak to the assistant manager, Christiaan van Niekerk, he's my cousin."

Over dinner, the six of us sat around the table. We had booked the tickets for the morning: A Qatar Airways 23-hour flight with a two-hour stop-over in Doha. I then held court and outlined our strategy for the days ahead.

We would visit the offices in Cape Town and speak to the managers to confirm Muller's story; that the diamond had been in President Zimbala's possession and was not still locked away in the vaults at the Head Office.

Once that had been confirmed, we would need to contact Muller and find out what he knows about Tomas Zimbala's whereabouts.

From what Mike Simpson had told us, we would then need to move to Mozambique, set up a base, acquire the equipment needed to carry out the operation, track down the man, and plan the heist.

Daniel was impressed, although Aunt Catherine could not believe her ears.

"It sounds like something out of a Le Carre novel, or what Ian Fleming might have written. Are you four serious?" she begged in disbelief.

"You're forgetting, Aunty, carrying out missions on foreign soil is what Alex, Jason, and I used to do for a living. That's why we sign the Official Secrets Act when we join Special Ops. The only difference is that this time we're doing it for us, not the Government."

It was late, and we needed to get some sleep; we thanked them and went up to our respective guestrooms.

Daniel had offered to drive us to the airport in the morning. It was a ten o'clock flight, so we needed to be there for check-in at six; it would be an early start.

We thanked Daniel as we bundled our bleary-eyed bodies out of his Bentley, retrieved our baggage from the boot, and entered the airport.

Perth Airport was all hustle and bustle again in this post COVID era. International flights resumed as though nothing had happened, despite the millions of lives that it had claimed over a two-year period. The only evidence remaining was the vaccination stamp on everyone's passports, and most people preferring to wear face masks in and around the airports.

8.30am, and the tannoy called us to the departures lounge.

10.10am, we were in the air and on our way to Africa; there was no turning back.

***

Book 2: Africa

Chapter 1

There was little in the way of conversation during our flight. Jess and I sat together, the other two a few rows behind. Not knowing what lay ahead, we all tried to get as much rest as possible.

Two hours before landing in Cape Town, we were woken from our slumbers to be served a breakfast of sorts. Jess then opened up the inflight magazine and told me all about the city.

"Did you know that Cape Town has a population of nearly four million and is the second largest city after Johannesburg? Also, the seat of government, where the South African Government meets."

"Thanks Jess, but I think that I already know that," I replied with a yawn.

"And that in 2014 they named it as the best place in the world to visit."

"That really is very interesting. However we're not here on holiday. There's a city map in the centrefold. We would be better studying that than the tourist attractions."

"Sorry brother, I was just saying."

"No, I'm sorry, I always get grumpy when I've been sleeping on a plane." I apologised. She was right. All local information is useful, and you never know when it might come in handy.

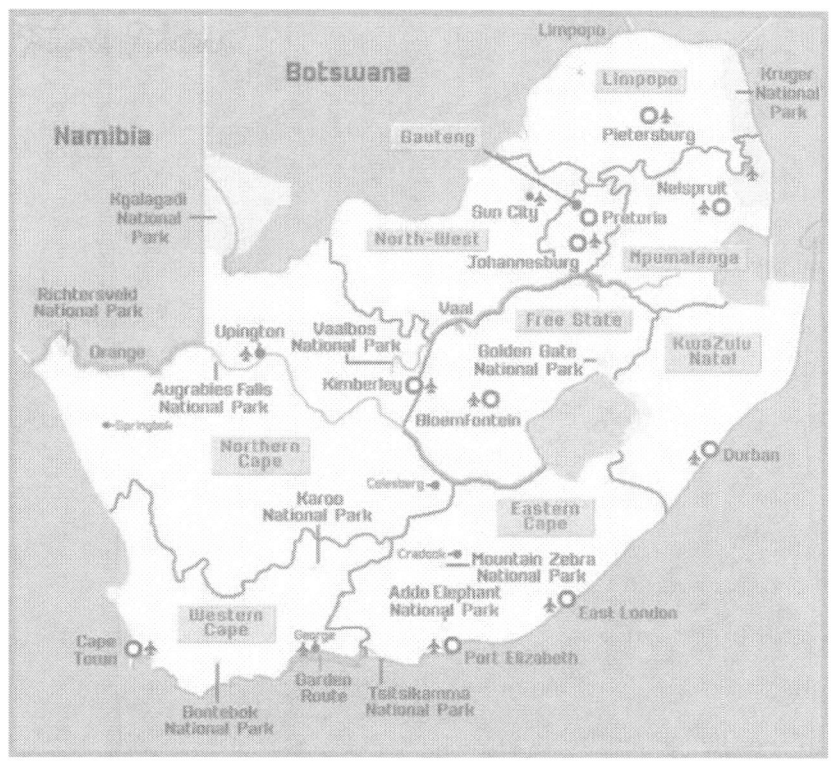

We had booked ahead into a small quiet hotel overlooking Lagoona Beach. It was inexpensive and a short drive from the centre of the city. By mid-day we had settled; a bite of lunch and all took a long walk on the beach as we made our plans for the next day. I needed a good night's sleep and a clear head before visiting the mine's headquarters. Also, and more importantly, I had to contact Kurt Muller.

Back at the hotel, I rang the number that Major Simpson had given me. It went straight into answer, and I left the message as instructed by Mike.

"Hi, I'm here in Cape Town from Australia on a sightseeing trip and seeking a reliable guide. Please call me back if you have any recommendations."

Now all we could do was sit and wait.

An hour later, I received a very brief message from Muller, who spoke in a thick Afrikaans accent that I could hardly understand.

"Cape Town is ok for tourists, but you'll prefer the climate in Johannesburg. Ring me when you get here." And he broke off the one-way call.

"A bit rude," commented Jess.

"No. All phone calls are brief and to the point, names are never mentioned; it's what we're taught to do," I explained.

"That would account for your lack of calls home over the last few years," she sarcastically responded.

At that moment, Alex and Jason entered our room.

"Any news from Muller?" was the first question.

"Yes Alex, we will meet him in Johannesburg. First Jess and I need to visit the Offices in the city."

"Shouldn't we all go?" he asked.

"No, it needs to be a casual visit; tourists tracing their family heritage, we don't want to attract attention to ourselves. You and Jason can get yourselves a bit of beach time. We'll meet back here for dinner this evening."

The taxi dropped us outside the 'Diamond Tower'; a glass fronted multi-story skyscraper. We took the lift to the fifteenth floor and knocked at the door with the embossed plaque which stated — "Kgomo Kanata, Vice President, Cape Town Diamond Corporation."

His secretary offered us coffee as we sat and waited.

Twenty minutes later, an elderly gentleman emerged from the inner office.

"I apologise for keeping you waiting. I see you've had a coffee; please come in," and he led us into his large gleaming, but minimalist office, where we sat at the cold-looking glass conference table.

Jessica introduced us and informed him she was writing a family memoir and was researching the history of Grandfather Joseph.

He smiled fondly at the mention of Joseph's name and invited us to move to the other end of the office to sit on the more comfortable lounge seats.

"Yes, I knew him well. I started working for the van Vuuren Mining Company as a young man and Joseph taught me everything that I know."

He then recounted his time working there when the Offices were an impressive, though smaller stone building. The many kindnesses that Joseph had shown to him and many of the others employed by the company. Finally, the sadness at the passing of Joseph in 2005, and the government taking control and renaming the company.

Kgomo ordered some more coffee, as Jess took copious notes and concluded by asking the question that had gone unexplained.

"That's fascinating, but what happened to the 'Star of Hopetown'? Is it still on display? I would love to see it." She enthusiastically asked.

There was a long pause. I could see the old man's eyes reddening, then he reluctantly replied.

"It was on display for many years, although when we became a nationalised company, they removed it from the offices to a safer place."

"So, where is that place? I'd love to see it before we return to Australia," she pressed.

"We are not sure. At one time, President Zimbala had it in his Office for visiting dignitaries to admire. Since they ousted him at the last elections, it seems to have disappeared; no one knows where it is." He rose from his chair and took a furtive glance out of his office door, then returned, and in a secretive fashion told us what he thought.

He recounted the time that father and Aunt Catherine had visited the offices, shortly after Joseph's death, and how the then government officials had refused to listen to their claims. He doubted that the current president would be any more inclined to hear them; it was too long ago, and much water had passed under the bridge since then.

Where the Star of Hopetown had gone, he could not say. Though like many others suspected, Zimbala had taken it when he fled the country to the sanctuary of his friends in Mozambique.

Kgomo made us promise not to mention his name in any memoir. If Zimbala ever returned, and there was a real possibility that he might, he would seek retribution upon anyone that had spoken out against him. That was a risk he did not want to take.

We thanked him for both his time and for disclosing all that he knew, and reassured him that his name would never appear in print.

On our return to the hotel, I noticed a tourist sign for charted trips in a light aircraft and could not resist the chance to see the actual mines, be it only from the air.

A trip that had taken our forefathers months to make, now covered in a matter of hours, and worth every minute. The Cape Town Mining Company was vast, covering an enormous area of open cast, and housing the deepest mine shaft in Africa. No longer prospectors sifting through the dirt and streams, the work now carried out by huge earth-moving machines.

The pilot circled the area for a second time, then headed back to the city airport.

After supper, we all returned to our room to plan the day ahead. I saw no need for us all to trip up to Johannesburg, which would only incur additional costs, so we decided I would go with Jason. If we got into negotiations about weaponry, he was the expert, and I did not want to get ripped off by Muller; Mike had already warned us that Kurt might push the prices up.

Surprisingly, there were no protests from Jess and Alex, who seemed quite happy to spend a day together as tourists and get in some more beach time.

I again reminded Jess that we are not tourists, and I wanted them to spend the day genning up on the departed ex-President Zimbala;

knowledge is power, and I needed to know everything about the man.

The following morning, Alex hired a car and dropped us at the airport for our two-hour flight to Johannesburg. Once we landed, I made another brief call to the number I'd been given.

"We've landed."

"Get yourselves a burger. Forty minutes," and he ended the call.

"That's great, there are hundreds of fast-food places, which one?" Jason scratched his head, then looked up at the massive, big yellow M. and added, "Is there anywhere on the planet where there's not one!"

We had already eaten before the flight; I ordered a coffee, but Jason couldn't resist a Big Mac; we sat by the window and waited. Thirty minutes later, there was a toot of a car horn; it was Kurt Muller in an old Toyota saloon, his head out of the driver's window and frantically beckoning to us.

"Jump in the back guys."

The engine was still revving, and he pulled away before any introductions were made. Once we were clear of the airport, he slowed, then stopped in a lay-by and turned to face us.

Muller was easily recognisable from Mike's photo. A giant of a man with a good head of blonde curly hair, the neck of an ox and a sunburnt face with a broken nose. The same age as Mike, but his lined weathered skin made him look several years older. He had been described as a hard man and first impressions left me in no doubt that he was!

"Sorry for the dramatics; there are too many cameras around the airport." He stretched out his massive hand. "I guess you must be Connor. Who's your mate?"

"Jason, he's come along for the ride."

"Well, from what Mike told me, it could be a bumpy one." As he said this, he gave a broad grin, exposing his shining gold tooth. "We'll head out to my place, where we can get some privacy."

He turned his back, switched on the engine, and we continued our drive out of the city in near silence. I exchanged glances with Jason; we were both initially impressed, but was Kurt Muller a man to be trusted.

Major Simpson had portrayed him as a wealthy man, an ex-secret service agent who had worked with the governments of two countries. Yet here we were, being chauffeured by this scruffy-looking Afrikaans in a beat-up old Toyota.

Thirty minutes later, we were being driven through a wooded area, then along a gravel track to a secluded house. The double doors opened as we approached, and Kurt drove straight in and parked alongside a gleaming Mercedes.

"You can leave your bags." It was more of an instruction than an offer, and we followed him into the house.

Inside, two of his associates, both large Africans, smartly suited, who stood at the door and never spoke to us.

"If you don't mind removing your jackets, gentlemen." Kurt politely asked.

We took off our jackets and stood spread-eagled; we knew the form. One of his men stepped forward and patted us down, to ensure that we were neither carrying guns nor wired up.

"They're clean."

"Thank you Matthew." And the man returned to his post at the door.

"Sorry about that, but I can't be too careful. Now take a seat, and what can I get you to drink?"

"Water will be fine," I replied and attempted a friendly smile. We took our seats on opposite sides of the coffee table. I glanced around; it was a beautifully furnished room. Mike had not been wrong as they settled into the elaborate chestnut brown, leather wingback, Chesterfield armchairs; Kurt Muller was a man of some wealth.

"So, what is it you want from me?"

A tricky question that I needed to answer carefully; I took another sip of water.

"I think that we may have a common interest," I tentatively opened. "What do you know about Tomas Zimbala?"

"Quite a lot, but what's your interest in the man?" His dark eyes were now focused and staring straight at me.

"I believe he has an item of property that belongs to me, and I have every intention of retrieving it."

"There's no need to be coy. Mike Simpson has already told me all about the Diamond. The question was, what do you want from me?"

"Ok, I know that you're trying to run down the billions that Gadhafi shipped down to South Africa before his demise, and that you are now working for the Libyan government to reclaim the money. The common denominator is Tomas Zimbala. You believe he has the money, and I believe he has my diamond. What do I want from you? That depends on what you know, and what aspirations you have." I took another sip, sat back, and waited for his reaction.

He said nothing; stood up and poured himself a whisky.

"You've been a busy boy, certainly done your homework." And he returned to his seat.

"Yes, I was working for the Libyans, on a 10% finder's fee. But the goal posts have moved; I'm now working for our President here; we have our own arrangement."

Am I allowed to ask what that is?" I hopefully enquired.

Again, he looked at me long and hard. I could see he was weighing up whether he could trust me.

"My only interest is the diamond. If I can help you, then surely that's good for both of us," I urged.

There was another long pause.

"Matthew, you guys take a walk and take Jason with you." Kurt instructed his men.

Jason gave me a cautious glance as the three left the room.

"Are you sure you don't want a scotch?" Kurt asked as he poured another.

"No, I'm still good with water," I lied; at that moment I would have killed for a proper drink.

"The arrangement with the President, was originally for me to track down the money, but not to return it to the Libyans. He offered me 15%, so I agreed; I'd be a fool not to."

"You said 'originally', so what's changed?"

"Zimbala is in exile in Mozambique. We believe he's in Maputo, although that's still to be confirmed. The word is that he plans to use the money to finance his return to power. My brief has now changed. The President no longer wants the money, but definitely doesn't want Zimbala to have it."

"So how do you plan to do that?"

"One large bomb should do the trick, and there will be a bonus should Zimbala get caught in the blast."

"That sounds fine for you, but what about my fucking diamond!" I was now on my feet; I had not come all this way to be told my dreams were about to go up in smoke.

"Sit down tiger, you haven't heard me out. If you come on board, you'll get your diamond; stop panicking man."

"What do you mean, come on board?" I was furious, stuff the water, I went and poured myself a scotch; Kurt gave a little smile.

"Relax, enjoy the drink, and hear me out. There is no reason why we should not work together. I need to recruit a foreign team to carry out the mission. And Mike spoke highly of you and your two friends. I have the Intel and you guys have the experience to pull off a successful operation. I believe your mate Jason, is the explosives expert, and I'll provide all the equipment that you need. Come on Connor, what do you say?" he urged.

I sat down again, staring into my glass. It was not an unreasonable request but didn't guarantee that I would get my hands on the stone.

"I can see that it's a splendid plan from your side of the table, but how does it help me get my diamond?"

He picked up the bottle and topped up my glass.

"I've a few ideas, don't worry on that count. I wouldn't fancy your chances of success without my help; so, are you in or out?"

He was right, we would be running blindfold with no access to equipment, and none of the background information stored in that enormous head of his; I had no choice.

"Ok, I'm prepared to listen. We'll carry out the job, but not before I have the diamond. No diamond, no assassination!"

"That's the right answer Connor. Invite Alex and your sister to join us here for a few days and we can discuss our ideas then. I've plenty of rooms and a pool in the back. See it as a brief holiday before we dispatch Tomas Zimbala."

He held out his hand and gave a toothy smile.

***

Chapter 2

The next morning, Kurt sent Matthew to collect Jess and Alex from the airport.

It was midday, and after they had made the introductions, Kurt suggested that we all relaxed around the pool before lunch.

He seemed to have undergone a personality change since our first meeting, all smiles, and no grimaces. Jess and the boys seemed to have taken to him, although I still had reservations, and hoped that we were not being played by the cunning old bugger. Expecting us to carry out his dirty work and assassinate Zimbala, with no guarantee of getting the diamond. Well, he said he had a plan, so I was looking forward to hearing it; it had better be good!

"Come on Connor, don't just sit there looking so serious, get your swimmers on and join us." Jess called from the water where she was splashing about with Alex.

It was ok for her; at this stage she did not know what we were getting into; or what dangers lay ahead. Although you would not think so by how Kurt and Jason were sitting in front of the television, watching the replay of the Springboks match against the touring British Lions from the night before. The pair with a beer in hand, excitedly shouting at the rugby players on the screen.

Later, we all sat indoors around the dining table. The housekeeper served up the meal, which mainly comprised of varieties of meat and more meat. It was little wonder that their rugby players appeared so tough, if this is what they all lived on.

Kurt continued in his happy frame of mind, and he stuffed more meat into his mouth, though all the time I felt his eyes were constantly watching me; I felt that he still had not decided about me.

I also had my doubts; I would not be happy until I had his trust and knew that I could trust him.

"Brandy anyone?" Our jovial host was full of 'Bon Ami', and obviously wanting to impress his guests.

I declined the offer and stuck with the wine and Jason with the beer, but both Jess and Alex were quick to join Kurt as he poured out three large glasses.

Why should this concern me? The pair had already had a skin full and were becoming a bit giggly and slurring their words. I did not want to become a killjoy, and on any other occasion this would not have bothered me, but with so much at stake, there was no time for a display of their childish behaviour.

"Sister, can I have a word?" I discreetly invited her out onto the veranda.

"Yes brother," and she reluctantly followed me outside.

"I don't know whether you've got a thing going with Alex, and I don't really care. But this is neither the time nor the place. So, for God's sake, leave it out until we get back to Queensland. We've got a job to do; we're not here to party!"

"Sorry, little brother," she slurred and slumped against my shoulder, tears running down her face. "Do you know how long it's been since I was in any kind of relationship?"

"I'm sorry too Jess, I don't begrudge you having a good time and Alex is a good man, but please, please save it until we get home. We all have a job to do, and I need you sober and focussed, just until it's all over. Can you do that for me?" I pleaded.

"Yes Connor; I promise, we'll not let you down." She wiped her eyes, and we returned to the dining room.

We will not let you down. She was already talking as if they were a couple. Maybe that would not be such a bad thing after all.

The light was now fading; the party was over and time for bed. Tomorrow would be an important day; decisions had to be made. What was Kurt's strategy, and would we still be working together by the end of the day?

The next morning, we all gathered in the kitchen for breakfast.

"Good morning my Ozzy friends, how are the heads?" Kurt cheekily asked with a grin.

"All good," I confidently replied, although I was not sure about Jess, who was wearing a pair of large dark glasses.

"Great, well, get stuck in. There's plenty of bacon on the go. Just help yourselves. We'll have a team talk after you have eaten."

Team talk? Apparently, Kurt Muller had made his mind up; I would wait until I heard what he had to say, but it was looking promising.

The meeting took place in the dining room, where Kurt had prepared for a briefing. His laptop connected to the enormous television screen displaying an enlarged picture of Ex-President Tomas Zimbala.

Like a college professor, Kurt gave us a lecture on the political situation in South Africa; including the recent elections where

Zimbala was ousted from power, amidst many accusations of corruption. The day after they announced the results, Tomas Zimbala disappeared along with the contents of the Treasury Warehouses, driven away in army trucks, by his loyal supporters. The vehicles allegedly carried stashes of bank notes that had been deposited in the treasury by the late General Gadhafi, reputed to be the equivalent of two billion in US dollars.

"I have tracked down Zimbala. He is now in Mozambique, living on an estate in Maputo, which has recently had two large warehouses constructed at the rear of his mansion." He clicked his Power Point presentation to the next picture, which was an aerial view of Maputo, then a closeup of Zimbala's place.

"I thought you didn't know exactly where he was living. How come you suddenly know about his mansion and the warehouse?" I asked accusingly.

"Steady Connor, don't be naïve. Surely you did not expect me to reveal everything at our first meeting. You're a stranger to my world. All I know is what Mike Simpson told me about you, and some of that was not very pretty."

Yes, I'm sure Mike would have told it, warts, and all. This was no time for me to take the high ground.

"Fair comment Kurt, please continue."

"Ok, so we know the general layout from satellite images, but we are still too short of reliable intel to safely make an assault on the place at this stage."

"I thought you said you had a plan."

"What we have in our favour is Zimbala's vanity, and at the moment he's courting as much publicity as he can, we believe that this is in the lead-up to his attempted coup, he has the finances in place and is feeling pretty cocky about his chances of success. And yes, I have thoughts of a plan." He refilled his water glass.

"Don't keep us in suspense," urged Jess.

"Well, it involves you Jessica. If you and Alex were to pose as foreign journalists and give him a sympathetic ear, we might get you inside the mansion for an interview, and a good look around."

"What would I be looking for?" she asked.

"Don't worry, Alex will know. All you have to do is keep his attention; butter him up as much as you can. Alex will just be your camera man and hopefully record as much logistical information as necessary for us to complete the operation."

"But what about our diamond?" I demanded.

Kurt just smiled and took another sip.

"If Tomas Zimbala runs true to form, he'll behave in the same way as he did when President. Apparently, he loves to show off his prized possession, The Star of Hopetown. If he doesn't, then maybe it's not there."

"That's not something that we want to contemplate. Everything is telling us he has it," insisted Jess.

"Well let's face it guys, the only proof of its existence are some photographs, the word of Kgomo Kanata, an old guy who despite being Vice President of the mine, is probably in his dotage and the memoirs of an elderly aunt, plus a lot of anecdotal hearsay. Yes, we know it existed, but who can say where it is now."

"Thanks for that Kurt. You really know how to inspire your team. So what's to stop us from walking out on you?" and I rose from my seat.

"Don't go throwing your toys out of the pram, just calm down and hear me out."

Calm down, I was furious. Had Kurt been conning us all along?

"Listen, I'm sure that Zimbala will have it, and if he hasn't got it, the game is still not over. What we definitely know is that he literally has a shed load of money; two sheds, to be precise. Yes, we plan to torch them; but what's stopping us from liberating a few bundles before we do; we could walk away with millions."

Kurt was right, Jess and I might be chasing an unattainable dream, but at least we would not be leaving empty-handed.

I looked at the other three.

"Are we still in?" I asked.

They all nodded in agreement.

"We have come this far, so why not?" said Alex with a sigh.

"I've no objections to a million-dollar payday," grinned Jason.

"It's not as though we don't need the money, but the diamond is what we came for, and I don't want to return home without it. If Zimbala doesn't have it, then someone else has, and we're going to get it," insisted Jess.

"Cheer up Connor, I was only being the Devil's advocate, I'm sure the diamond will be there," and Kurt stood up and held out his hand; the game was on!

"Ok Kurt, let's talk logistics."

***

Chapter 3

We spent the rest of the day drinking endless cups of coffee, as we firmed up Kurt's ideas.

First, the journalists.

Kurt requested Jess and Alex's passports; he had a man in Pretoria who was an expert in producing documents at his request. As usual, good men didn't come cheap, and two days later, they had reproduced the passports at a mere ten grand each. Julia Anderson and Adrian Davies, both Freelance Journalists, working for the Australian Times magazine. A convincing legend, and letters from fictitious editors, and a stamped business visa.

Jason and I accompanied Kurt to visit Isaac Jacobs, an elderly gentleman whose frail appearance and failing health belied his hardened core, the most ruthless arms dealer on the continent of Africa. With the perpetual coups and wars, Isaac was never out of work and cared little for which side he was arming, often playing both sides against the middle.

After a long discussion, Jason and Kurt agreed their shopping list.

Semtex 10 explosives, the first choice for most terrorist organisations. Isaac boasted he had friends in Libya, and access to the stocks brought into the country by the late General Gadhafi; he could get us as much as we wanted.

Automatic weapons: He tried to sell us the Russian AK47s. The cunning old Jew probably had a surplus supply he needed to move, but Jason was having none of it; he preferred the German Koch 36, also the Beretta M9, and was insistent. One Remington 700 sniper's rifle, two handheld Bazooka rocket launchers, a dozen grenades; Jacobs promised that we would have the delivery in ten days.

Eventually the deal was done, and handshakes made. I went away happy and relieved that I had brought Jason along to fight my corner.

With the weaponry and documents sorted, it was now time to move onto reconnaissance, transportation and, most importantly, our exit strategy.

The Intel that Kurt had gathered had come mainly from satellite images and from bribing one of the staff working at Zimbala's mansion. We knew the two warehouses were guarded 24/7 by at least four armed men. The perimeter was enclosed in a barbed wire electric fence and had a pack of Doberman Pincers running loose to discourage any unwanted visitors. This was not something that we were going to rush into; Jess and Alex's visit and information gathering would be vital to the success of our mission.

Transportation would not be a problem, as the President had promised Kurt, that he would have unrestricted access to the military's transport, this gave us the use of an Army Boeing Bell Helicopter, plus pilot, but with all of its South African military insignia removed.

A safe exit was the one thing that concerned every member of the Special Services. Getting in and taking your target by surprise was rarely a challenge, however getting out in one piece was often a different proposition.

The range of a Bell Boeing Osprey is a little over a thousand miles, so on completion of the mission, our choices were limited. South Africa could not be seen to have any involvement in the assassination of Zimbala, so Kurt definitely did not want us to return to him.

We studied our options; Kurt suggested Madagascar. It was only a 700mile flight from Maputo and he had connections in Toliara on the south-east coast. The chopper could drop us there, refuel and return to Johannesburg, leaving my team of terrorists to sail off into the mist in a boat provided by him. Then we only had to navigate across the Indian Ocean, and we were home!

It sounded like a simple plan when it came out of Kurt Muller's mouth.

We would take out the guards, neutralise the dogs using steaks and the dart gun, assassinate Zimbala, collect my diamond, blow-up the warehouses and his mansion, be picked up by the chopper, flown to Madagascar and make good our escape, SIMPLES!

Did I have any reservations?

Of course, I bloody well did!

I had no doubts that we could carry out the assignment; we were seasoned campaigners who had been trained for these types of covert operations.

It was all a matter of trust; and the question still was, could I trust Kurt Muller?

Once we had taken out Zimbala and his crew, then torched the place, what guarantees did we have that the Helicopter would collect us on time; or at all.

Then there was the possibility of us walking into a reception committee from the Madagascan Army.

Was I being paranoid? Jess and the others seemed happy in Kurt's company. Maybe it was just me.

Then there was the problem of navigating our way across the Indian Ocean; apart from going fishing in a tinny, none of us knew anything about sailing, let alone navigating across four and a half thousand miles of open sea.

A simple plan in theory. If any of the four of us knew anything about boats; but we didn't!

Kurt could see the anxious look upon my face and discreetly took me to his study.

"What is it Connor, are you having second thoughts?"

"Why should I? you seem to have all the bases covered, so what is there for me to worry about?"

"You don't fool me, I can see that something is bothering you, so what is it?" he asked as he placed his arm around my shoulder.

"Do you really want to know?"

"Yes, of course I do, Connor; we are all on the same team."

"Are we?" and I pulled away from him. "I'm taking all the risks with no guarantees, but from the moment I kill Zimbala, all your objectives will have been achieved and I will have served your purpose."

"Oh, ye of little faith; chill and have another drink." The concerned look on his face morphed into a wide grin.
"Look, Connor, if you're having doubts about my commitment and loyalty to the mission, then I'll send Matthew in with you while Jessica can stay with me and keep out of the firing line. Would that make you feel happier?" he asked.

"I suppose so," I replied, we returned to the lounge and poured another drink. There I explained my concerns about escaping via the Indian Ocean; surely there must be a safer and quicker way of getting home.

He assured me that the best way of getting back into Australia unnoticed, with a stash of cash and diamonds, would be by boat, and I was not to worry; the boat would come with an experienced skipper.

Kurt seemed to have all the answers, which was easy for him; he was in a win-win situation and not the one that would risk his life in a gun battle.

Anyway, we were now all committed to our course of action and the clock was ticking!

***

Chapter 4

Monday 01.30 hours.

We all climbed into the rear of the Boeing Bell, and the pilot fired up the blades. The deafening noise eased as we cleared the wooded area and lifted into the moonlit skies above the low-lying clouds.

It was an uncomfortable flight for Jess, who had never been in a helicopter; and spent most of the journey clutching Alex's hand.

We flew through the night and put down in the semidarkness just as the sunlight broke over the distant hills. The pilot landed the helicopter at an opening near to a semi-derelict farmhouse; an isolated spot two miles outside the small town of Mbuzini, close to the border with Mozambique, and a four-hour flight from Zimbala's mansion near Maputo.

We set up camp in a secluded farmhouse just outside the small town of Mbuzini, near the border of Mozambique and a 700-mile flight from Maputo. We entered the old building and set up a temporary lighting system from our portable generator.

The inside of the cottage was covered in dirt and dust. It appeared to have been abandoned for many years, although there was evidence of the previous occupants; a few pictures still hanging on the walls, one or two knickknacks on the shelves, all the cupboards and food stores were empty; it was obvious that they had left in a hurry.

All our equipment, the weapons, basic food supplies, clothing, and bedrolls were stored in one backroom. Jess cleaned and organised the kitchen whilst Alex got the stove going. Matthew,

Jason, and I helped the pilot to construct a crude covering for the helicopter, to hide it from any prying eyes.

Kurt naturally assumed the right to be the Commander-in-Chief and sat in the kitchen chatting to Jess, while the rest of us tidied up the other rooms, as this would probably be our barracks for the next seven days.

Four hours later, all the chores were sorted and the seven of us sat around the table on makeshift boxes and benches, as Jess served up a brunch of bacon and eggs.

We spent the rest of the day studying maps and firming up our strategy.

Tomorrow we needed to contact Zimbala and sell him the story of the journalists from Australia. Kurt had already spoken to Mike Simpson; it would sound more authentic if the call came from Australia, and he purported to be the magazine's Editor. If Zimbala bought the story, the next step would be to get Jess and Alex into Maputo, then into Zimbala's mansion for the interview. But with an eight-hour time difference, we would have to be patient and wait for Mike to get back to us.

As the evening approached, I proposed the sleeping arrangements; it was a small cottage with limited space and options, so Jason and Alex would have to share a room, Jess and I would take the other bedroom, Matthew and the pilot had offered to sleep in the chopper, which was probably more spacious and comfortable than any of the rooms in this old building, that just left Kurt to rig up a bed for himself in the kitchen.

Jess vetoed my suggestions, stating that she would prefer to bunk in with Alex, which came as no surprise, although I didn't fancy sharing with Jason; you could hear his snoring from a hundred meters away.

Kurt fetched out a bottle of Brandy after the evening meal and suggested that we might like a nightcap to help us get to sleep, with all the creaking timbers inside and various animal noises outside; he was obviously missing the comfort of his luxurious home.

Tuesday, 07.00 hours, I awoke to a text message from Mike.

"His press sec would be delighted to receive our two reporters. They seem keen to welcome any media from abroad that will give Zimbala a sympathetic ear. They're still claiming that the election was rigged, and that Tomas Zimbala is the rightful President of South Africa and would soon return."

Mike had done a good job. All Jess and Alex had to do was to keep Zimbala sweet, whilst they had a good look around; and hopefully discover the whereabouts of our diamond.

Jess telephoned the number that Mike had given us, and the press secretary made an appointment for the following afternoon. This gave us time to get them into a hotel in Maputo; equip them with a camera, recorder, and notebook so that they would convincingly look the part.

The pilot flew them to a small village outside Maputo that had a railway station; a quick drop off and the chopper disappeared into the low-lying cloud. The pair then boarded the next train into the city, and at midday booked into a hotel under the names of Julia

Anderson and Adrian Davies. Confidently, they produced their passports bearing the occupations Freelance Journalist and Photographer, respectively.

They spent their afternoon shopping and mingling with the locals, as any journalist might. Of those they spoke to, most had never heard of, or showed any interest in Tomas Zimbala, but of those who had, he was just another corrupt politician that their government had let into the country.

The following morning, they phoned the Press Secretary, who offered to send a car to collect them after lunch.

Wednesday 14.30 hours.

The large electric gates swung open, and the armed guard waved them through.

The black limousine came to a halt at the steps of the mansion, where they were greeted by the Press Secretary who was wearing a smart pin-striped suit. Zimbala stood at the top of the entrance steps, wearing his colourful Chieftain's robes.

They warmly exchanged introductions and handshakes.

"I thought my traditional robes would look better on any photos that you will take," he explained as he led them into his library; he was keen to impress upon them he was an educated man, that had been to Cambridge University in England and not an "Uneducated Gangster," as he described the current President.

They sat on the leather upholstered sofas, and made polite conversation, whilst the maid served afternoon tea in bone China cups.

Tomas Zimbala did not portray the image the Jess had expected, neither in appearance nor speech.

On photographs, he appeared to be a large imposing figure, but not so in the flesh. He was not very tall and had small, fine facial features. His body shape undefined as it was hidden under the robe. They say that the camera never lies, but I guess it depends on the angle at which the picture's taken.

His voice was soft, and he spoke with an articulate English accent, with no hint of Afrikaans. Jess could not imagine him on the podium, shouting and rallying the troops.

She was finding it hard to accept that this was the man they had come to assassinate.

Alex, on the other hand, had no such qualms and was busy making mental notes; the security cameras, the number of staff and how many of them might be armed. So far, he had seen no evidence of the guard dogs; maybe they were only let out at night.

Jess carried out the interview, as though she was a professional that had been doing it all her life, while Alex took several photos of the pair happily talking together, with the massive bookshelves as a backdrop.

Zimbala insisted to the reporters that this was to be the people's revolution and he had no plans for a military coup and would only return at his people's insistence.

The reporters were lapping up his propaganda and continued to adopt a policy of flattery.

Alex admiring the beautiful architecture of the mansion. Claiming to have been an architect prior to becoming a photographer, asked if they might show him around the rest of the building.

Tomas agreed for his secretary to show him around, whilst he continued his conversation with Miss Anderson.

When Alex and the secretary had left the room, Jess moved seats and sat closer to Tomas; they were alone, so this was the time to broach the subject of the diamond.

"Rumour has it you possess the largest diamond in the world, is that true?" she asked, with a wide-eyed look of anticipation. "Any chance of seeing it?"

"It's true that I have the 'Star of Hopetown' if that is the one to which you refer, but it is only one of many in my collection. Unfortunately, I cannot show you. The collection is locked away until I return to Pretoria. When I do, it will be back on display, and I will send you a personal invitation to come and admire it."

A broad boastful smile had appeared on his face at the mention of the diamond; these were the words that Jess was waiting for. She now knew where the diamond was.

Alex returned twenty minutes later after his guided tour, which included the outside area, where he could see the dog pound and two large, newly constructed sheds.

"What's kept in the sheds?" he innocently asked the secretary.

"Nothing really, just odds and ends of farm equipment."

Farming equipment my arse, Alex had noticed the reinforced doors and coded security locks, also the man casually sitting on a nearby bench, with a semi-automatic rifle across his knees.

Alex had seen as much as he needed to. It was time for them to make their retreat.

Before they departed, Miss Anderson assured Tomas Zimbala she would personally email him the proposed copy and photos for his approval before the magazine went to print.

***

Chapter 5

Thursday 13.00 hours.

Jess and Alex had returned from Maputo, and we all settled around the kitchen table for the debriefing.

"Ok Alex, let's have it," urged Kurt. "Tell us what we're up against."

"Well, I was lucky enough to get a full guided tour," Alex said with a smile. "I don't envisage that we will meet with too much resistance. I only saw two armed guards, if I can call them that, both sloppily dressed and carrying ancient looking automatic weapons. One was stationed in a hut at the entrance, the other by the sheds. I would be more concerned about the dogs. I saw half a dozen of them in the pound; those Doberman Pincers look vicious. The devil dogs have been known to tear a man to shreds." He said with a shiver.

"What about surveillance equipment?" I asked.

"A random selection; at the gate and the entrance door, interestingly they were mainly concentrated around the sheds at the rear; I think that's telling us something. There is a small bank of screens in a room on the ground floor."

"What about the domestic staff?" asked Kurt.

"No more than a dozen, their quarters are at the rear on the ground floor."

"Make sure that they come to no harm. The chef is my man on the inside," Kurt informed us.

"Zimbala's rooms are on the first floor; let's hope he is a good sleeper. At four in the morning, it should be a doddle!" Alex sat back, pleased with his work.

"And the sheds, do they present a problem?" I pressed.

"Electronic locks; child's play. I'll have them open in a jiffy," he boasted.

"Well done Alex, a good day's work. Anything to add Jessica," Kurt asked.

Jess had sat patiently; she was bursting to impart her piece of news.

"I'm almost certain I know where the diamond is," she excitedly proclaimed. "Tomas Zimbala admitted to having it, and assured me it was somewhere safe, so it has to be in one of the warehouses."

Her enthusiasm waned when she spoke of her interview with Tomas Zimbala.

"Is it really necessary for us to kill the man? He seems a reasonable, well-educated man who deplores violence. Can't we just take the diamond and burn his stash of money?"

"Are you kidding?" exclaimed Kurt. "I was in military intelligence when he came to power. The man's a megalomaniac. You might think it a coincidence that most of his opposition party met with unfortunate deaths, but I can assure you that none were accidental!"

Jess sat open-mouthed at these revelations; she had been totally taken in; Tomas had seemed such a nice man.

There was a long pause as all the information and disclosures were digested.

"So where do we go from here?" Jess asked nervously.

"We go hard and fast. We have all the intel and nothing's likely to change; the sooner the job's done, the better." It was time for me to rally the troops. It would be a dawn mission and I would need until Friday to finalise the details.

We drew up a checklist, while Jess made the lunch and Matthew went out to the helicopter and retrieved a large sack, which contained a selection of combat clothing, all South African military with all the badges and insignia removed.

The helmets came with integrated headsets and there were several pairs of boots in varying sizes; it felt like we were at a church jumble sale as we rummaged through the sack, trying on whatever fitted.

It was easier with the balaclavas; one size fitted all.

Next the explosives; we had planned two for each of the warehouses and another two for the house. Jason carefully separated the Semtex into six packages, then counted out the six charges and timers.

We stripped the firearms, cleaned, and reassembled them, each of us taking responsibility for his own weapons, an automatic rifle and side-arm. Jason lovingly removed from its case the Remington sniper's rifle, taking his time in checking the sights and the night vision scope. I could swear that the man was in love with that gun. It was the model that he had used in Afghanistan on many occasions.

I did not know whether he would need it. Jason always favoured killing at a distance, but I feared we would have little choice; it would most likely be at close quarters this time.

The last pieces of equipment were the six empty kit bags, that would hopefully contain the proceeds of our mission.

Friday 10.00 hours.

Kurt went outside to make another call to his mate in Madagascar, the one with the boat. They were talking for some time, which was unusual for Kurt, who was normally a man of few words.

"Everything ok?" I enquired.

"Sure man, all's good. Larry just wanted to know a little more about his passengers and their cargo."

"So how much did you tell him?"

"Don't worry Connor, I only told him as much as I had to."

"Which was?" I asked accusingly; I was not happy with Kurt's explanation.

"Listen, Larry and I go way back and have helped each other out frequently. When he retired from Military Intelligence, he followed his love of sailing and eventually bought the 'Dream Star', a ninety-foot yacht. It's an ocean-going vessel, and he has used it occasionally to top up his pension, running a little import, export business."

"Good for Larry, but you haven't answered my question."

"Ok, I had to tell him something. So, I said that you and your pals are smuggling a few diamonds into Australia. I've made no reference to Zimbala; honest!"

I was not totally happy with Kurt's excuses, but he was right. This Larry character was bound to ask why we wanted to take a pleasure cruise across the Indian Ocean.

"You haven't mentioned the price."

"Larry settled on the cost of four first class flights; twenty grand in US Dollars. If all goes to plan, you should have that as loose change in your pockets. Treat this as another brief holiday; three- or four-weeks' pleasure cruising across the ocean."

I think that Kurt should have been a politician. He never answered a question directly and always seems to put a positive spin on any given situation.

We would set off in the middle of the night. I wanted to hit our target at 04.00 hours, while most of them would be asleep. I suggested we try to get a bit of shuteye, although I knew it would be almost impossible, given our uncomfortable accommodation, added to the fact that we would go into combat in a matter of a few hours.

The bright searchlight from the helicopter shook us from any slumbers, then the whirling sound as the pilot started the engines.

Five minutes later, all our goods were stowed on board. The last task was completed when Alex and Jason had disconnected the generator and put it into the hold, then buckled themselves in; we were ready.

I pulled the side hatch closed, and we slowly lifted off into the night sky.

***

Chapter 6

Saturday 03.45 hours.

We could just see the lights from the city centre of Maputo. They appeared to twinkle like fairies, inviting us towards our destination.

The pilot hovered at the far side of a small scrubland area a kilometre from the mansion. Even in the semidarkness, I could see that Jess's eyes were welling up, and that she was putting on a brave face to fight back the tears. There was a kiss on the cheek for me, and on the lips for Alex.

"Good luck. Come back in one piece; I love you," her voice was cracking as she choked back the tears and withdrew to the darkest corner of the cabin.

This was no time for sentimental indulgence, and the four of us checked each other's equipment before climbing down from the craft. Kurt carefully passed the box containing the Semtex to Jason, who took one handle and Matthew the other, to ensure a smooth transfer to our target.

"Do you have everything?" Kurt called down to us over the noise of the whirling blades. My brain was racing; I struggle to run through the list in my head.

"Steaks," I called, "the bag with the steaks and darts."

He tossed the bag to me.

"Good luck, we'll be back here at 0600 hours; try not to be late guys." A smile and feeble attempt at a joke, but I would not expect less from the old campaigner.

We quickly moved clear of the downdraft as the Bell lifted into the air. A short trek through the scrubland and we would be at the mansion.

They had forecast that there would be a full moon, but a thin layer of low-lying clouds only allowed minimal light for us as we stumbled through the undergrowth.

Eventually we came to the clearing, and the mansion stood silhouetted against the skyline. We lay in the long grass, less than a hundred meters from the entrance gates.

We scanned the front of the building with our night vision glasses. I could see the guard in the small wooden shelter. There was no sign of any movement; his head slumped forward, he was asleep at his post, which was no surprise; I checked my watch; it was 04.15 hours.

We waited another 5 minutes; still no movement, so we pulled down our balaclavas and edged forward towards the gates.

"Lose the guard Jason." An instruction that gave me no pleasure; killing in combat is all part of the game, but shooting someone who is defenceless leaves an unpleasant taste.

Jason attached the muffler to the Remington, one shot from less than 50 meters, and the man's brains were splattered over the wall of his hut.

The electric gates were easily short-circuited by Alex, and as we quietly pushed them open, we heard the dogs bounding towards us. We quickly pulled the gate back, and I pulled the meat from my bag.

"Here doggies, good doggies," and I threw pieces of the steak towards them, which they instantly devoured, then tentatively approached us at the gate, looking for more, which I gladly gave them whilst Jason silently put them down with the dart gun. I looked at his sad face, how strange I thought, that a man can kill another without the slightest remorse, yet when he puts down a pack of dogs, it is with a heavy heart. Hopefully, we would only kill one more creature today.

We split up and circled the building from both directions. There was no sign of the other guard; like his colleague, he was probably asleep somewhere.

I again checked my watch. It was 04.40 hours; the clock was running against us. I told Jason and Matthew to keep looking for the missing guard; we didn't want any sudden surprises.

Alex and I silently crept into the building. The door to the control room was open, and the missing guard fast asleep in front of the screens; one blow to the back of his head from the butt of Alex's gun and the man was no longer a concern to us.

Then up the stairs and into Zimbala's suite of rooms.

As we entered his bedroom, he stirred from his sleep.

"Who's there? Who is it?" he sat up in the bed and reached for his glasses.

As he fumbled to put them on, I stepped forward and fired two rounds into his head, the exit wounds spraying blood over the bedhead.

The deed was done in silence, now we needed to create noise and panic.

We burst into the staff quarters, discharging our guns into the ceilings, shouting, and screaming at them to get up out of bed. It was their worst nightmare come true.

We herded them into the main entrance hall, where Matthew addressed them in the local dialect to avoid any misunderstanding.

"Tomas Zimbala is dead, and this building will be raised to the ground in twenty minutes. You have until then to collect your belongings and leave unless you wish to be cremated with him. Now go!"

There was no doubt that Matthew's message had got through. Within minutes they were scuttling away down the drive, into the light of the breaking dawn; running for their lives to escape the threatening monsters.

It was now 04.55 hours.

Once we were certain that the building was empty, we raced to the sheds; Alex worked his magic, and the doors swung open. We weren't sure what we were looking at; in the middle of the shed were a stack of pallets, each wrapped in several layers of cling-wrap. Matthew stepped forward and ripped open the first bale, and pulled out a fistful of hundred-dollar bills.

"Shit man, how many pallets are there?" he could not believe what he had in his hand. None of us had ever seen so much cash in our lives.

I threw the empty kitbags to Jason.

"You and Matthew fill these."

"How much Connor?"

"Don't ask stupid questions. Ram as much as you can into them. Alex and I are going to see what's in next door," and left the pair, frantically stuffing the bags.

By comparison, the other shed was nearly empty, apart from a single pallet in the middle of the room.

I carefully peeled back the wrapping; there was a selection of small polished wooden boxes and one large chest. One by one, I examined the boxes. Each had various names inscribed on the outside. Then I found it, the Star of Hopetown.

I slowly lifted the lid and laying on a velvet cloth was the glistening stone; beautifully cut facets reflecting every ounce of meagre light in the shed; how good would it look in the full light of day? I stood mesmerised by its beauty.

"Buck up Connor."

Alex had shaken me from my trance. It was now 05.15, and we still had to lay the charges and be back at the rendezvous at 0600.

The chest bore the stamp mark of the "van Vuuren Mining Company." I cautiously raised the lid to reveal a layer of uncut stones. They varied in size and looked more like translucent pebbles than diamonds.

I placed the smaller boxes in the chest.

"This is coming with us Alex; have a rummage around, there must be a trolley or wheelbarrow somewhere."

While he searched, I ran to see how the others were progressing with the bag filling.

"Nearly done. Give Matthew a hand while I sort out the explosives." instructed Jason.

"Ok, no need to blow the one next door. It will be empty when we leave. Just do this one and the mansion."

05.25 hours; time was running out.

As Matthew and I carried the bulging bags out of the shed, Alex met us, pushing a gardener's wheelbarrow with the chest precariously balanced on top.

"Set to blow in 30 minutes. I just need to rig up the mansion, so you guys start heading back. I'll catch you up."

"No way Jason, I'm coming with you, these two donkeys can make a start, we'll soon catch them up."

Alex pushed the barrow with a kit bag over each shoulder, while Matthew's large muscular frame managed the other four bags.

We carried the rest of the Semtex into the hallway and Jason made one bomb; he inserted the detonator and attached the timer; the explosions would go off simultaneously and would certainly be heard in the centre of Maputo, some ten miles away.

It was now 05.45 hours.

We sprinted out of the building and retraced our track through the undergrowth. The sun appeared over the horizon, and our pathway clear; we could see the other two ahead of us, struggling with the barrow, their helmets discarded and sweat running down their faces.

"You two have taken your time, turning up once all the hard work has been done." Alex looked exhausted, and a bit pissed off.

"Stop whinging Alex and move out of the way."

Jason and I grabbed a handle each and lifted the chest from the barrow; only another couple of hundred meters and we would be in the clearing.

06.00 hours and we collapsed into a heap; four spent bodies gasping for air after our mission.

In the distance we could hear the faint whirring of the Boeing; five minutes later it was hovering above us.

As they came down, Kurt and Jess had their heads sticking out of the hatch. She then gave Kurt a hug of joy; we had all returned with no casualties.

Alex and Matthew climbed aboard, and we tossed the six bags up to them, then carefully passed the chest containing the diamonds before getting in.

"We got it Jess! It's ours! The Star of Hopetown is ours!"

"Show me, show me," she excitedly asked.

"Wait until we're clear," I attempted to calm her down.

"Never mind the diamond, what about Zimbala?" demanded Kurt, as we lifted into the air.

Before I could answer, there was an enormous explosion; debris flying high into the air, small pieces narrowly missing us as we climbed into the sky.

"Does that answer your question?"

"And the man himself?"

"Don't worry, the President will happily pay your bonus; if they ever find Zimbala's body beneath all the rubble."

"Cheers Connor; a good day for all of us. With a sack full of cash each, we are millionaires. You and Jess have your diamond, plus some, and I'm still to receive my rewards from our President."

The pilot reached cruising speed and headed due East, his coordinates leading us to Madagascar and our journey home.

"Can I see the diamond now, brother?"

"Sure." I smiled and raised the lid of the chest.

***

Book 3: Going Home.

Chapter 1

The mission had been accomplished; Kurt Muller was correct, we were all now millionaires, but there were no popping corks; this was not the time. We were all exhausted from the physical and mental stress that had been put upon us; the celebrations would come later.

The flight to Madagascar was a quiet affair, apart from Kurt constantly disappearing in and out of the pilot's cockpit to make and take calls. I guess that was to communicate the details of our success to his employer, and to ensure that he would deposit Kurt's due rewards into his bank account.

The morning sun was glistening on the water as we spotted the coastline of Madagascar.

The pilot circled the city of Toliara, then swung south along the coast until he came to the small coastal village of Lanantsony; a collection of shacks with a few larger houses close to the ocean.

We landed in a large sandy paddock at the rear of one house and waited until the blades stopped turning and the dust had settled before we slid open the hatch doors and climbed out of the helicopter.

Kurt was greeted with a manly embrace from Larry, he then introduced him to the rest of us.

They were an unlikely-looking pair; the bulk of Kurt's muscular frame, standing alongside this skinny little man, whose dark, almost black weather-beaten skin could not hide his delicate features.

Laurance Bartholomew had more the look of an accountant or clerk than either an Intelligence Officer or a hardened seaman. Still, as I have learnt; you should never judge a book by its cover.

It was lunchtime; Larry invited us to sit under the shade sails, out of the sun, which was blazing down upon us. He handed round the cold drinks, and a young man came out of the house and lit up the BBQ.

"Come and say hello Dominique," and called him over.

"This is Dom, he is my," and he hesitated, "He is my, my companion."

Well, we all knew what he meant; Dom was a pretty young man and at least forty years younger than Larry; Hell who's judging; certainly not any of us who had committed murder a few hours earlier.

"What happened to the last one?" I heard Kurt ask quietly.

Larry pulled him to one side; I never got to know the answer.

"Do you guys want to stow your things in the house? We'll eat in an hour, and maybe you'd like to shower and change out of your combat fatigues. The war is over," our host offered with a friendly smile.

The problem is that when you are carrying a fortune, where is the safest place to leave it? I knew that Kurt, Matthew, and the pilot would leave once they had refuelled the Boeing Bell, and that we would put out to sea the following day; I had no choice, so we moved everything from the helicopter.

It felt good to get out of our dirty battle dress and back into shorts and tee shirt. All the borrowed uniforms, helmets, and boots were squashed back into Matthew's sack and put back on board.

"What about the weapons?" asked Kurt.

"We have no use for the grenades or automatic rifles, but I know Jason has become attached to the Remington and wants to keep it. As for the side arms, I think it best to hang onto them until the voyage is over; I'll dump them when we're back in Australian waters."

"That makes sense; you've a long journey ahead."

The shower felt so good; cold fresh water washing away the dirt and sweat, sadly not the guilt of the mission; no one likes to think of themselves as an assassin or murderer.

During the meal, I had the uncomfortable feeling that we were being watched. Then a sigh of relief, as I realised we were merely being observed. Not by the military, but by a gang of young children peering over the wall. They had never seen a helicopter close up, only the ones flying high in the clouds.

After we had eaten, Matthew and the pilot refuelled the helicopter from the tanks that Larry had stored in his shed.

1700 hours, the sun was going down, we could see the beautiful red sunset across the water; it was time to say our goodbyes to Kurt, Matthew, and the pilot.

We stood well back as the chopper lifted, spraying dirt and gravel as it ascended into the evening sky.

We returned to the lounge, and I handed Larry a large brown envelope.

"Half now, half when we're in Australian waters," I stated in a business-like manner.

"Sounds good," and he peered into the envelope. "Time for a drink. Now what will it be lovey, bubbly, beer or brandy?"

Bubbles for Jess, beer for Jason, a large brandy for Alex and I stuck with the sparkling water. I liked our convivial host, but I intended to stay sober and would keep a pistol under my pillow tonight.

***

Chapter 2

The following morning, I awoke early as the sun rose. I had little sleep during the night; surely, I was not the only one to have been kept awake by Jason's snoring.

But no! Everyone else at the breakfast table said that they had heard nothing; I guess they had other distractions.

Once Dom had cleared away the dishes, Larry spread his charts across the table.

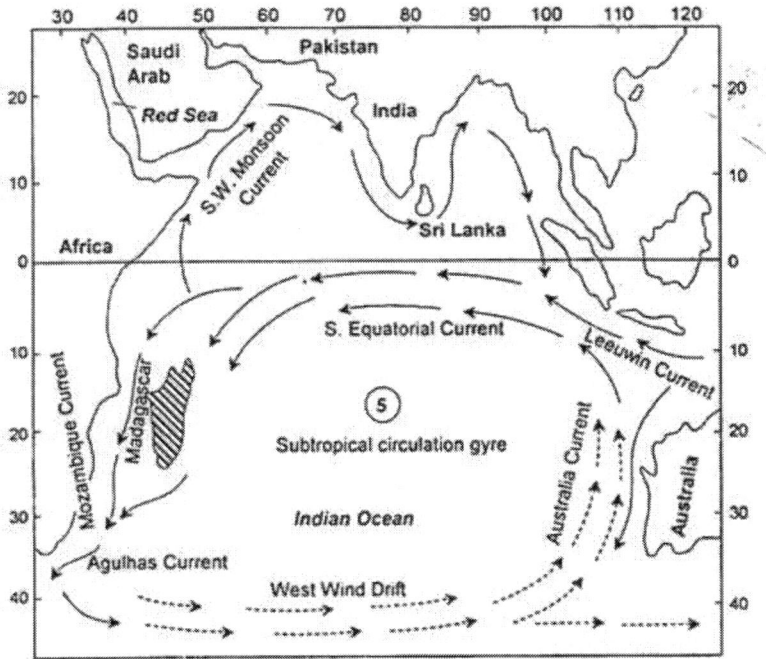

"Ok guys, listen up. I'm hoping to set sail at high tide, that means 1500 hours to you non sailors. I hope you all have good sea legs. You are going to be on board for six to eight weeks, depending upon the sailing conditions."

"How long?" exclaimed Alex. "Kurt told us it would be a four to six-week sunshine cruise across the Indian Ocean. We hoped we might stop off at Mauritius or the Cocos Keeling Islands en route."

A big grin appeared on Larry's dark face.

"Sorry, but we don't go anywhere near either of those two places."

"What the hell are you talking about? Call yourself a sailor; look at the fucking map for God's sake. Take a straight line from Madagascar to Australia and any fool can see that we could call in at one of them with a brief detour."

Both Jess and Alex had taken Kurt at his word and thought that this was going to be plain sailing; a luxury holiday for them.

"Let me give you all a lesson on sailing. You obviously know as much about it as my good friend Kurt."

He then delivered the lecture.

Explaining that; a sailing vessel relies upon the wind and currents to get from A to B. Yes, his yacht has a diesel motor, which is strictly for emergencies, and anyway it could never carry enough fuel to make such a crossing.

We could attempt to sail north then east, which on the plus side would be warmer; but there were two factors which ruled that route out. One that we would sail against the South Equatorial Current, which flows from east to west. The other reason being that there was always the chance of encountering pirates and the further north we go, the more likelihood that they could attack us.

"So my friends, the route that we will take is to head south, then pick up the West Wind Drift. It's quicker, safer, but I must warn you it will be much colder, and certainly no pleasure cruise."

"Surely the closer we get to Australia, the warmer it will be?" asked Jess.

"The East Australian Current flows north to south. That's why Queensland's waters are so warm. But with the West Australia Current, it flows from south to north. Does that answer your question Jess?"

Reluctantly, we all had to accept that Larry was the sailor; not any of us, so we would go in any direction that he took us.

Mid-morning and we were instructed to gather our belongings together as one of Larry's neighbours pulled into the backyard in an old truck.

"Throw your things in the back and climb on board; it's only a short drive to the jetty."

At the small harbour there were a variety of sailing vessels, the largest of which was the 'Dream Star.' Kurt had described the ninety-foot yacht to me, which did not make it sound very large, but I was pleasantly surprised to discover that it was a lot bigger than I had imagined.

It was an ocean-going vessel, with six berths, shared equally between three cabins, and had a decent sized galley.

We stowed our belongings in the lockers located under each bunk. I had reminded my team that most people can resist anything but temptation, so we wanted neither Larry nor Dominique to be aware of what was in the kit bags; yes, they knew about the diamonds but not the cash, and it needed to stay that way!

Above deck, the boat had two enormous masts that seemed to go on for ever as I stood beneath them looking up to the heavens and praying for good weather.

We all helped to load the provisions into the hold below deck. It would be a dry trip in terms of alcohol; water was not an issue, as the yacht had its own desalination unit built in. Boxes of dehydrated goods took up most of the space, and Larry assured us that food would not be a problem; provided that we all like fish.

Finally, we took on board our supply of diesel for the engine, hoping that it would not be needed too often.

15.00 hours and under Larry's instructions, we cast off. Using the engine, he skilfully navigated us out of the shallow harbour and into the depths of the Indian Ocean.

Once we were clear, he cut the engine, and we hoisted the sails. For the first time in my life, I experienced the thrill as the power of the wind thrust us through the water.

Jess and Alex together at the bow in their shorts and tee shirts, enjoying the wind in their faces and sat holding hands; maybe it would be a pleasure cruise for loves young dreamers.

Our skipper had set a course SSE, and within a couple of hours, the southern tip of Madagascar was disappearing behind us into the darkening of the night.

We decided we would share the night watches in pairs, the first night being taken by Larry and Dom, while the rest of us retired to our cabins and attempted to sleep despite the motion of the yacht.

The end of day one, but it felt no closer to home; Africa was behind us, but Australia seemed a million miles away.

***

Chapter 3

The first week passed without incident.

We had all established our sea legs; taken turns at keeping watch and duties in the galley. Jason and Dom seemed to be born anglers, providing us with an abundance of fish, which we had fried, grilled, baked, and boiled.

It was still warm enough to wear shorts and take the occasional dip into the ocean when we dropped sail and drifted for a while. Larry, who insisted that we stayed attached to the lifeline at all times, strictly supervised these leisure activities; he had never lost a passenger in the past and had no intentions of losing one now.

A few days later, we picked up the West Wind Drift. There would be no more dips in the ocean, the tee shirts replaced by windcheaters and sweatshirts. Not only a noticeable change in temperature, but the wind and size of the waves had increased considerably.

I felt anxious, as the water was rising higher than the bulwarks and washing across the deck. Jess and the boys were fooling around having fun in the spray, unaware of my thoughts and fears.

Their fooling about ended abruptly, when Jess was nearly washed overboard by an enormous wave; Alex instantly joined her body, dangling over the side as she desperately clung on to the rails in his reckless attempt to save his lover.

It took the combined strength of Jason, Dominique, and me to drag the pair back on board. This larking about and comedy of errors had nearly taken the lives of the foolhardy pair.

The rough, dark seas became illuminated as the lightning flashed across the sky and the angry waves smashed against the side of the boat, turbulent and unforgiving, rocking the boat to a tipping point.

The storm's tempo had risen at an alarming rate; from calm to wild within a matter of seconds and we slipped and slid our way below deck to the safety of our cabin; every sense of the pattern and direction lost'. It would be Larry's skill and the compass that would get us through this; I had become totally disorientated.

Not only the noise of the storm outside, but the water barrels rolling from side to side, cooking utensils rattling and adding to the confusion and mayhem. Any unsecured belongings, bouncing and rolling about into the cabin area between the bunks.

Jess was now taking the voyage seriously; I caught her sending up a quiet prayer to the Almighty for protection.

I was about to join her, when there was a sudden loud crash; it was something on the deck and water swept into the cabin where we were all huddled together. The terrifying look on our faces sent Larry out on deck to examine the vessel. Our captain showed as much courage as any soldier on the front line as he braved the storm above decks.

We were afraid that the little lightweight, might get washed away, but after a few minutes of dreading the worst, the hatch re-opened and he returned with another deluge at his back, to inform us it was only a flimsy part of the bulwark which had broken off; it had caused no serious damage.

It was all hands to the wheel as he handed out the bilge water pumps and buckets. It was like trying to push water up-hill, a nigh on impossibility, but we eventually made progress and went from knee deep to water covering our ankles.

We felt we were winning the battle against the elements, unaware that there would be an even more powerful gust that would batter us with full force.

The boat was being tossed like a cork, at one stage smashed flat into the water, sails, and all. We clung together, shaking, and petrified; but slowly the boat came about; up righted and ready to start all over again.

Except for Jess and Dom, we had all encountered danger and terror: we were experienced veterans who had fought in Afghanistan, but this storm at sea had induced fear and danger that we had never known. We had no control of the heavy dark clouds that loomed overhead; the lightning and sound of the waves crashing, or the uncontrollable fear that gripped us.

At the end of the third week, what had been our sense of fresh air and freedom turned into restraint and confinement as we spent more time below huddled together in the one dry cabin. The games of cards and Larry's game of Trivia initially kept us entertained, but at the end of the third week, we were all stir crazy and getting on each other's nerves. The least comment from anyone sparking off another vindictive argument.

The storms eventually eased; we had all survived, albeit battered and bruised. Thank God none of us had suffered seasickness. That was until the middle of week four; Jess had been looking pale, and I caught her throwing up over the stern of the boat.

"What's up Jess? Lost your sea legs?"

"No brother," she replied as she wiped her face with a hand towel. "I don't think its sea sickness. I have also been feeling emotional, dizzy, and exhausted. Have you not noticed? What do you think?"

"No, surely you're not. Are you?"

"Yes, I think that you're going to be an uncle."

"But how? Sorry, that's a stupid question. What I meant to say was when." I naively asked.

"It was the night we were at Kurt's place."

"You mean a drunken fumble that went wrong?"

"No, you idiot, we are in love. Don't you dare talk like that, just because you have got no one."

I immediately felt ashamed of my last stupid remark and apologised yet again; will I ever learn not to keep putting a foot in my big mouth!

"Sorry Jess, that came out all wrong. Alex is a great guy; I know you will both make wonderful parents."

I lovingly put my arms around her, whilst trying to keep my balance as the yacht listed from side to side in the wind.

"Let's go below and celebrate. I can't imagine that Larry has not got a bottle stashed away somewhere."

Dom stayed at the helm while Alex summoned the rest of us down to his cabin to impart their good news.

When pressed, Larry admitted he had a bottle of brandy in his cabin, which he kept strictly for emergencies; well, I guess that on this occasion he classed this as a type of emergency.

A small tot for the boys, but Jess satisfied herself with a cup of tea.

Larry then toasted the couple.

"So Larry, as the captain of this ship, do you have the authority to marry this happy couple?" teased Jason.

Joking apart, I could see that this was going to be no picnic for Jess if she continued to have morning sickness, afternoon sickness, middle of the night sickness, and the cravings. The weather warning on Larry's radar was forecasting storms. It would be another rough ride ahead in all senses of the word. Jess would be the primary concern, as she was constantly tired and needed rest.

Two days later, we were amid one more raging storm; it was all hands-on deck, as Larry had us all reining in and securing the sails.

There was nothing else that we could do but sit out the storm and pray to God that we came through it at the other end. All the millions that we had stashed below would count for nothing if we all finished up as shark bait.

Dom had secured all the loose items in the galley; cooking or preparing any type of meals had become an impossibility. We were once again reduced to hard tack biscuits, water, and vitamin pills for the next twenty-four hours.

The next morning came the calm; the storm had spent its energy. There had been minimal damage, some water in the hold and the engine room, and both masts had survived the ordeal. On this occasion, once again, God had been on our side; we had a boat that could float, and no one was injured. Throughout the mayhem, Alex had adopted the nurture phase, as he lovingly cared for Jess and her unborn child.

The others raised the sails, though progress was slow. We were hardly in the doldrums, but it could have seemed that way as we slowly drifted in the right direction, with the sails hanging loosely. Each new day was a new start, a new sense of normal, as the feeling of reality shifted upon its axis for Jess and Alex. She sat in the sun and felt warmer for the growing belly she constantly cradled.

The ecstatic joy of coming through two horrific storms relatively unscathed, now replaced by the frustration of making so little progress.

"Is it time to use the engines?" I asked our captain.

"Maybe tomorrow. Let's wait and see before we go burning the diesel."

"For fuck's sake Larry, what's the point of having an engine if we don't use the bloody thing!"

"Steady down Connor. This yacht only has one captain, and that's me. If you don't like it, I'll inflate the dinghy and you can paddle your way to Perth. Is that what you want?"

"No. I'm sorry Larry, I know you can't fix the weather, it's just the claustrophobia; all of us being jammed together like a can of sardines is driving me crazy. Will we ever reach Perth?" I asked in frustration.

"All the money in the world will not get us there any faster; we will arrive when we arrive. So, if there is nothing else? I have got jobs to do."

And he disappeared down the hatch and into the small engine room, leaving me full of steam and nowhere to blow it off.

The tight little weasel had mentioned 'All the money in the world'. Did he know something; had he discovered what was in our kit bags; or had Muller told him the full story?

Yes! that was a possibility; all these spooks tend to share their secrets and I had never liked the look of Kurt Muller from the start; but what could I do about it?

Warn the others to be on their guard, or possibly we could do what they did to Captain Bligh on the Bounty and cast him and his boyfriend off in the inflatable.

Yes, that's what we will do. We all know how a boat works; it cannot be too difficult and I'm sure we could manage without happy Larry, anyway Alex will know how to sail the damn thing.

Alex? If he's getting together with Jess, they will have over two million between them. Is that why he was so keen to get her into bed? Had he planned the whole thing?

Jess, however, would be oblivious to Alex's thoughts; wrapped up in her feelings for the unborn baby, her precious child, one conceived in perfect love.

I had better warn Jason. Jason? Why did he insist on keeping the Remington? Was he planning on assassinating all of us; he would have four million plus all the diamonds.

Was there anyone that I could trust? Maybe they were all in it together, and conspiring to get rid of me?

All these questions and doubts chasing wildly through my brain. I felt dizzy, my head tilted back. I stared up at the lifeless sails, which had spun around and around.

I desperately reached out for the rail but missed, staggered, and fell.

***

Chapter 4

I awoke two days later, lying on my bunk: Jess wiping the sweat from my brow.

"Sit up and try to drink some soup."

"What happened Jess?" I asked and attempted to raise my head from the pillow.

"Larry found you collapsed on the deck. Lucky we were drifting, otherwise you could have been washed overboard."

My mind was a blank. I had no recall of falling or hitting my head.

"Are we nearly home yet, Jess?" I pathetically asked as a small child might to its parent.

"Larry thinks that if the wind holds course, we could be in Perth within ten days." She sat me up and held the mug of soup to my lips, without spilling it; the weather had obviously improved. We were sailing along smoothly instead of being tossed all over the place.

Ten days from home, it was time to formulate a plan; just how were we going to get the money and diamonds into the country undetected.

The Australian Border Force, the agency responsible for offshore and onshore border control enforcement, investigations and compliance, pride themselves on the record against drug dealers and smugglers.

It had been no trouble getting in and out of Africa, but Australia was a different proposition and would take considerably more thinking about.

I finished the drink. I needed to freshen up and call the troops together for some brainstorming.

But should I include Larry; I still had my doubts about him, although a man with his background could prove useful.

He was at the wheel checking our course. I casually sidled my way beside him and enquired about the weather, then slipped in a question about Kurt.

"Did he tell you about the deal he had with the President, concerning Gadhafi's billions?"

"Don't you mean Zimbala's billions?"

"Yes, I suppose so," I replied, as if I had no real interest.

"Connor. I can read you like a book. What you are really asking is, 'Do I know about your stash?' and I'm not referring to the diamonds."

I felt my face reddening; it was clear that he had been a top man in his field of intelligence and had sussed me; I turned and looked him straight in the eyes.

"Well, do you?"

"Of course, I do. Please don't take it personally, but I would take no one on board without knowing what they were carrying. Do not worry, I have nothing against smuggling, but I draw the line at drugs; if I thought that was the case, you and your friends would never have put foot on my yacht."

I had been wrong to underestimate the man and would have been a bigger fool not to have him on my team.

I thanked him for his openness and apologised for my behaviour two days earlier.

"Think nothing of it. Cabin fever is not uncommon on such long voyages, anyway we will soon have you home."

About home. I would value your input. We're meeting to decide the best way to avoid the Border Agency. Any ideas you have would be welcome."

"That's not a problem; ask Dom to come up here and stand watch. I'll be with you in a few minutes."

The five of us sat discussing various ideas and could not decide, so drew up a short list.

- The old lobster pot trick of wrapping them in watertight material, throwing them overboard to be collected at a later date.
- Getting a tinny, put in a false bottom to hide the goods and deliver them to a quiet spot.
- Employ a Sea Plane and parachute the goods to a deserted spot inland.

All three suggestions had merit; Larry had sat in silence and not said a word.

"Come on Larry, what do you think?" urged Jess.

"Yes, those ideas might work, but they are old hat; the Border Force would be wise to all of them."

"So, what would you suggest?" I asked.

"Ok, it's not something to rush into. What's the hurry? You don't need to get them all in at the same time. It will have taken us eight weeks to complete our journey. What difference would a couple more weeks make?"

"None whatsoever Larry."

"Good. So suck on this one." Larry then gave us a master class in smuggling.

"The best way to pass through customs and check points unnoticed, is not to either wear disguises or try to avoid being stopped and possibly searched. No, it's becoming a regular face; a face that eventually blends into the background." He paused for a sip of water, and to check that he had the full attention of his audience.

"Always engage with the officers. They have a name on their badge, so use it. Smile, chat and pass the time of day, offer to show them what's in your bag or vehicle." He took another sip; I could see that he was loving being the centre of attention.

"It might take several dry runs before you are ready to move any goods."

"But how will we know when the time is right?" I asked. These ideas were fine in theory, however at some point we would have to put it to the test.

"Most small ports have the same officers carrying out the same tasks day after day. When they stop calling you sir, or madam, and start using your first name, you know they are dropping their guard. And that's the time to make your move." His presentation was over, and he was ready to take a bow and the plaudits.

"Thanks Larry, that was fascinating; exactly how often have you put your theories into action?"

"That would be telling Connor. Let us just say since I retired from the South African Military, I have kept myself busy," he replied and gave me a sly wink.

It had been an illuminating talk, although I still did not know how we were going to get the contraband ashore. The answer was sitting opposite me.

"The theory lesson was great, but would you be interested in helping us on the practical side of things?" I asked.

I really needed Larry to be involved all his years in intelligence, not to mention his post-retirement activities. Yes, I desperately needed the man; please say yes!

And I held my breath for his answer.

"Sure Connor. Not a problem. But firstly I need to know why Perth, the west coast of Australia is massive, so why Perth."

I gave him a brief explanation of how this whole saga started; Aunt Catherine's book and how her husband, Daniel van Niekerk, had financed the whole expedition. So our first port of call had to be Perth, where they live. Daniel would need to see the return on his investment.

Larry sat patiently and jotted a few notes.

"Ok, that sounds fair enough. Give me a couple of days to work something out; if you like my ideas we'll talk money."

More money? Oh well, the old saying *'Good men don't come cheap,'* certainly applies to Larry!

***

Chapter 5

For the next two days, we saw little of Larry who had locked himself away in his cabin, other than when he needed to check our course or stand his watch.

Day three, and he invited Jess and me into his cabin.

"Ok, moving the stones will be easy, but four million or more in hundred-dollar bills will take a little longer."

We sat on the bunk opposite him in excited anticipation, waiting for him to explain his master plan; this time there would be no interruptions.

Larry opened his notebook and worked his way down the list: -
1/ Daniel and Catherine; day at the beach.

"It needs to be somewhere busy with lots of people in and out of the water. Dominique will take you on the inflatable. Once you're close enough, you can swim to the beach. I'm assuming you can both swim." He glanced up from his notes; we both nodded.

"Good. Find aunt and uncle, dry off and go home with them."
2/ Rottnest Island; Birds.

"Have you heard of Rottnest Island?" he asked.

We looked at each other, then shook our heads.

"Well, it's a small island near Perth, designated an 'Important Bird Area', also famous for its population of quokkas, a small native marsupial found in very few other places. But it is the birds that we are interested in, they include the pied
cormorant, osprey, pied oystercatcher, silver gull, crested tern, fairy

tern, bridled tern, rock parrot and the reef heron; the list is endless. Is Daniel interested in birds?"

"I've absolutely no idea." At this stage, I could not see where his ramblings were going; maybe it was his turn to go cabin crazy!

"Well, I hope he is I've just upgraded him to Professor, and a respected ornithologist. You two will accompany him on his daily research trips to the island. There is a ferry service from Fremantle. They permit 4x4's on the island so you will need to get one, ideally with two spare tyres."

"What's with the tyres?"

"I don't know how many hundred-dollar bills you can fit into a deflated tyre, but you'll soon find out."

Genius! The man's a bloody genius; I could now see what he had in mind.

"And the diamonds, you said that would be easy." Jess needed an explanation.

"Diamond, Ice. Ice, Diamonds. A small fishing boat or tinny, with two Eskies, a couple of bags of ice and a few fish. I'm sure you get the picture."

Things sounded so simple; I could now see why I was a foot soldier and he an officer in Intelligence.

"What about Alex and Jason?" asked Jess. "Will they be coming with us?"

"That would be very trusting of you," he said with a grin, "I'm sure that you would prefer them to stay on board and keep an eye on your goods, anyway, I'll need them to ferry the goods to you on the island."

Larry had seemed to have thought of everything; although I knew that his expertise was going to come at a price.

"Cheers Larry, now what's it going to cost us?" I tentatively enquired.

"Well, you still owe me another 20k, so let's round it up to a nice 100. What do you say?"

I had no choice; I couldn't do it without him, and it wasn't as though we didn't have the money.

"Ok. Let's call it a deal," and held out my hand.

Two days later we were in Australian waters, and I replaced my sim card tossing the obsolete South African one into the sea.

It was time to ring Daniel.

Both he and Catherine were ecstatic at all the good news, the retrieval of the Star of Hopetown and the chest of uncut stones. However their excitement dampened when I related the story of the money.

Daniel said that the assassination of Ex-President Tomas Zimbala had made the news. The newscaster had stated that a terrorist organisation from Mozambique had claimed responsibility for the attack.

Terrorist organisation my foot!

I smiled; this story was obviously the work of Kurt Muller, the cunning old fox.

I then briefly outlined the plans to Daniel as to how we would retrieve the money and diamonds; I would text the details once we were closer to home.

It would be plain sailing now, or so I thought.
Mid-morning, an inquisitive helicopter circled us. Jess and Alex, who were sunning themselves on deck, casually waved to the pilot, who turned the chopper and headed for the mainland.

Larry immediately pulled out his binoculars.

"Shit, that unmarked chopper will belong to the Border Agency; we can expect a visit within the hour."

"How do you know that? It could just as easily be tourists on a joy ride," I commented.

"No. As soon as they see that we're not locals, and from overseas, they will send someone to look us over; it's time to tidy up below deck."

He called Dom to take the wheel, then summoned us to his cabin. He dismantled his bunk and moved it away from the side, then unscrewed the panel.

"Ok, collect all your goodies and stash them in here."

We immediately followed his instruction; he had obviously been in this situation before. We then helped him reassemble the bunk and returned above deck.

"Connor, the guns?" he asked.

"Fuck! I'd forgotten about our guns and Jason's Remington. I'll fetch them and put them with the rest of the things." And was about to dash down to my cabin.

"That's not an option, Connor; they'll have to go over the side. If they come aboard with a sniffer dog, it will soon find the firearms and your hoard of contraband. It's my neck on the block and not a risk I'm prepared to take. So, toss them overboard now!"

Larry was insistent; and he was right. I collected the firearms, but Jason was refusing to hand over the rifle.

"It's not a problem; I can just say it's for hunting. Many hunters use a Remington."

"Not a great excuse Jason, unless you can magically produce a bill of sale or a licence for the weapon. Sorry mate, it's got to go."

Ten minutes later, Jason fetched the gun case and handed it to Dom, who went to the stern and dropped it over the side, along with the three hand guns.

"Don't look so sad, Jason; you're a millionaire, you can afford to buy another when you get home." I tried to console my friend, who appeared distressed at the loss of his precious gun.

We then returned to the cabin to create the fiction of where we had come from and where we were heading.

Again, Larry was the one to come up with the bright ideas.

"Do you still have your papers from the trip to Africa?" he asked Jess.

"Yes, but how is that going to help us?"

"Ok, may I see them?" He studied the passports and work visas. All the time, I could hear his brain ticking.

"Once again you are Julia Anderson and Adrian Davies, both Freelance Journalists, working for the Australian Times magazine. It was a convincing legend with fictitious editor's letters. It worked well once, so let's keep it going." His worried face now relaxed as he explained his plan.

Anderson and Davies had completed their assignment, and decided that they would go on an adventure, returning across the Indian Ocean on a yacht; it would make a great article for the Magazine when they arrived home.

"That's great, Larry, but how do you explain the presence of me and Jason?"

"A simple part for you two, ex-marines turned beach bums; got into trouble with the police after a bar brawl in Joburg, made your way to the coast and hitched a lift back to Australia on my yacht."

"Do you think they will buy that?" I asked; it sounded far too simple to be plausible.

"Sure they will, just play the thick squaddie; it shouldn't be too difficult for the pair of you."

"Cheers Larry; I love you too!" The cheeky old bugger, but as usual, he was the one with the answers.

"Trust me guys, all that they are interested in is drugs, guns and illegal immigrants," he confidently assured us.

Twenty minutes later, we saw a motor launch heading in our direction; it would soon be time to put Larry's ideas into action.

Another thirty minutes and the large red vessel was alongside.

"Dream Star. This is the Australian Border Force," the captain announced over the speakers. "I am sending a boarding party. Please have your papers ready for inspection."

Four officers climbed out of the inflatable boat and stepped aboard. Larry introduced himself, and the officer inspected our papers and passports. After a cursory inspection, he radioed to his captain.

"Send Jasper over please."

Another inflatable arrived, this time with an officer and dog. Jasper was a scruffy-looking Spaniel, that once aboard had its well-trained nose into every nook and cranny.

Nothing had been found, so Jasper and his handler returned to the main vessel.

The officer in charge took me and Jason to one side.

"So where did you two serve?"

"Afghanistan, three tours, we came out two years ago." I explained.

"I was in the SAS until 2014. If you guys tire of bumming around the world, you could do worse than join this mob. Plenty of action and the pay's not bad." He was a friendly bloke, wanting to help old comrades.

We shook hands. He reminded Larry to log in when he reached Perth and to all our relief; they returned to their ship and moved on to the next call, having bought all of Larry's stories and found nothing.

***

Chapter 6

We were fifty metres from the beach when we carefully slid over the side of the inflatable, each clutching a small watertight bag containing a dry change of clothes; my phone and a few other essentials. We took our time as we mingled between the other bathers and surfers, while Dom discreetly drifted away, before heading out to sea and back to the yacht.

Eventually we lay on the crowded beach, having opened our bags, and spread our towels. Once we had dried in the sun, I rang Daniel.

"Where are you?" I asked.

"In the carpark back of the Surf Club."

I scanned the beach; I could see the sign for the club a couple of hundred metres away.

"Good. We'll be with you in five minutes," and ended the call.

We gathered our things and slowly made our way along the beach. It felt weird, walking on solid ground after eight weeks aboard a swaying boat; Jess' sense of motherhood, cradling her stomach, twice had to grab my arm for support.

In the Bentley sat both Daniel and Catherine. Aunty was full of questions before we had even pulled away.

"Could we leave it until we get home? I'm dying for a hot shower and a strong drink." I implored her.

"Yes, Cath, give the kids a chance to recover after their voyage. There will be plenty of time for questions and celebrations when we get in. Connor, I might even find you a razor."

I suddenly realised that I had neither looked in a mirror nor shaved for the last eight weeks; I must have been a scary sight!

As soon as we had walked through the door, Jess reminded me that neither of us had phoned mother. She and Patrick were relieved to hear that we had arrived back safely, ecstatic when we informed them we had the diamonds, and we were all now millionaires. If everything went to plan, we should be back in Queensland within two or three weeks; then we would celebrate our newfound wealth. Jess decided she would drop her own bombshell once they were home.

We put the phone down and I headed upstairs to my room; the luxury of a hot power shower after weeks of cold water coming out of a makeshift hose was indescribable.

Then steak and chips; instead of fish and more fish that had been served up in a hundred different, tasteless ways.

Ah, luxury!

It was great to be back in civilisation and in the comfort of their home; if I never stepped aboard another boat in my life, I would die a happy man!

Over dinner, all of Aunt Catherine's questions were answered, as she quizzed me over every detail from the moment we had left her home several months ago; the visit to the mine, meeting Kgomo Kanata the Vice President of the Cape Town Diamond Corporation, the mysterious Kurt Muller, our visit to Zimbala's mansion in Mozambique and finally the voyage across the Indian Ocean with Laurance Bartholomew, another ex-government agent.

I could not decide whether she was planning to write a sequel to her book, or a spy novel.

After dinner, we sat in the lounge, and I explained our plans in detail.

Daniel would pose as an elderly semi-retired Professor, Jess, and I as his niece and nephew, who were helping him with his book; "The Birds of the West Coast."

We would take daily visits to Rottnest Island from the ferry at Fremantle, in a 4x4.

While on the Island, the boys would take one of the spare wheels and stuff it with the cash; it would take several trips, including a few dry runs, to give us time to build a relationship with the staff at the port.

I then explained that Daniel would be a pivotal part of the entire operation. Not just in posing as a professor, also with his business connections, he could help us launder the money.

"And is there anything else that I can help you with today sir?" Daniel asked with a broad grin as he fetched the brandy bottle.

I could detect that both he and Catherine were loving the whole adventure.

It was then that Jess informed the family that she was pregnant. She touched on all the changes which had challenged her on the last leg of the trip; the growing discomfort and the emotional levels which she had suffered because of the hormonal changes. She was, however, determined to see the venture which they had undertaken through to the end. Aunt Catherine and Daniel were overcome with the news of welcoming a new baby into the family.

Chapter 7

The next morning was spent preparing for the trip to Rottnest Island.

Firstly, the permit; a little more involved than Larry had let on. It involved completing a lengthy questionnaire on conservation issues before being granted.

Then the vehicle; Daniel owned an old 1995 Toyota Land Cruiser, which he had not used for the past ten years, and was covered up at the rear of his second garage. We pulled off the tarpaulin to reveal the two-tone green and silver beast, which had the spare tyre bolted on to the rear. Fortunately, despite it not having been used for years, Daniel had kept it serviced and the Rego up to date.

He also owned an assortment of cameras and binoculars for us to choose from, so with that and a satchel full of note pads and reference books, we would look the part of a studious group from the university.

In the afternoon, I made a quick call to Larry, who had moored the Dream Star in the Fremantle Marina and logged in with the harbour master.

I informed him we were ready and would make our first dry run in the morning.

Larry would go on daily trips out to navigate around the island to identify any likely rendezvous areas.

That evening, as we sat around the dining table, I felt we were almost there, in recovering our diamonds and the bonus stash of money.

Aunt Catherine proposed a toast.
"Here's to you and Jessica, who succeeded where your father and I had failed. They proposed a further toast for the safe delivery of the new baby."

"You haven't failed Aunt. Without your book, Jess and I would never have gone on the expedition. So, cheers to all of us, and to you Daniel for financing the whole thing."

After we had eaten, we sat in the lounge with our brandy.

"Tell me more about my father. I was only thirteen when he died, and with him flying off to the mines for weeks at a time, I hardly got to know him."

"Well, my brother was much like you; hard working and tenacious. He didn't want to quit after our trip to Cape Town. We spent a fortune on solicitors, but the Government in South Africa would not budge and claimed that the mine and all its assets and possessions belonged to them. The legal wrangles went on for two years and we eventually had to give in; it was a fight we would never win."

"But we have now," I insisted. "It's just a small matter of getting it ashore."

The warmth and joy in the room at that moment in time filled us all; I only wished that my father was here to share it.

That night, as I tried to sleep, my mind kept returning to my father. It was not just how he had tragically died at the bottom of a mine shaft; but how mother had been forced out of our home, all because the owners denied all culpability and only paid a little in compensation; the bastards!

I could not sleep; I had righted the wrongs in Cape Town and now wanted to seek justice for the death of my father. I knew I needed to put these thoughts on hold while we finished dealing with our current situation.

As we joined the queue of vehicles awaiting the Rottnest Ferry, we were surrounded by numerous signs and posters regarding the conservation on the island; and a larger sign warning of the penalties for removing things from the Island, which included all plants, animals and especially birds' eggs.

The uniformed officer at the gate to the ferry was George Fergusson, a dry witless middle-aged Scot, with no sense of humour, who took great delight in questioning us about our visit and then pointing out the penalties, which were already clearly displayed.

"What a pompous little man," commented Daniel as I drove up the ramp.

"Strangely, no mention of either diamonds or bank notes, so we should be ok," Jess whispered with a giggle and a nudge as we drove on to the ferry.

The island was approximately 10 kilometres by four, so took us little time to survey the bays and coves, looking for suitable beaching areas for transferring our goods.

The north-west coast of the island looked most promising, with easy off-road access to the water, although I knew that the final decision would lie with Larry.

We spent lunchtime sitting on the cliffs eating the picnic that Aunt had prepared for us. In the distance, we could see a yacht coming into view.

Jess grabbed the binoculars.

"It's them!" she excitedly announced. Then jumped up and frantically waved.

"Sit down Jess. Two things sister dearest, one, they cannot see you from that distance, and second, we don't need to be letting the entire world know what we're up to. So, a little restraint please; you'll be seeing lover boy soon enough."

She reluctantly sat down like a petulant child and poured another coffee from the flask. She needed to contain her composure.

"Time you took a chill pill brother; don't you know how to have fun?"

"We'll have plenty of time for fun once the diamonds and cash are safely on shore. In the meantime, stay focussed on what we are doing. Anyway, I need you to have some fun with George; bring a smile to that miserable face of his."

The Dream Star soon passed from our vision, and we set about capturing a few photographs of birds.

A pied cormorant, osprey, an oystercatcher, silver gull, crested tern and a pair of rock parrot; yes, that should be enough to convince Officer Ferguson that we were on a serious assignment.

The sun was going down as I drove the Toyota off the ferry; at the gates stood George Ferguson.

He put his head through our driver's window to have a nosy. Yuk! I wasn't sure whether it was his bad breath or the smell of whiskey that was knocking me back.

"Would you like to check the back officer; I can assure you that all we are taking away are some photos." I forced a friendly smile.

"Yes. I'm not interested in your pictures, but I will take a look in the back laddie."

Jess could see that my attempted efforts were failing, so jumped out and swung open the large rear door. The officer, not noticing the bump, had a quick rummage, all he found beneath the blanket were a couple of spare cameras, a tripod, and our picnic hamper.

"Bye George, see you tomorrow," smiled Jess as she got back into the car.

"Ok, you're good to go; and it's Officer Ferguson, if you don't mind young lady." And he waved us through the gates.

"He looks like a dour old sod; are you sure you can win him over?" Daniel asked Jess.

"No worries, he'll be putty in my hands," she confidently replied.

And so it proved.

On the second day, we followed the same routine; this time with Jess at the wheel, radiant, all smiles and wearing a loose-fitting tee shirt.

"Morning Officer George, and how are you today?" she enquired as she smiled into his eyes.

"I'm good thanks, how are you?" as his face reddened slightly, and he attempted an uncomfortable smile, making no eye contact with either Daniel or I, then stepped back and waved us through to the Ferry.

"Have a good day," he called.

"You too, George," and Jess drove through to the ferry.

Later that afternoon, George Ferguson was still on gate duty as we drove off the ferry.

"We are all ready for inspection George," Jess announced as she wound down the driver's window.

"No need to get out miss; I'll just take a wee look." He opened the rear door to see the same assortment, the empty hamper and photographic equipment.

"So, how was your day? Did you discover any new species?" He asked in an attempt to show interest in what we were doing.

"Well, I must show you this picture of a nesting pair of Rock Parrots; my brother risked life and limb hanging over the cliff edge to get it."

She then held the digital camera out for him to see the nest.

"That's a great photo; what's your brother's name; Spider Man?" he joked.

Well, we call him Connor, though I do not know what he really does in his spare time, so he could be some kind of Super Hero." She countered with a grin. "Come on Connor, 'fess up, have you got another job?"

"Ho-Ho, very funny sister, as if I had the time with all your demands! If you have any sisters George, you'll know exactly what I mean."

"Aye, I do, but mine live in Scotland so they have spared me all that."

"You cheeky pair, I see that misogyny is alive and well in Western Australia."

"Sorry Miss; I was only joking," apologised the embarrassed officer.

"No worries George, so was I," she reassured him with a broad smile.

"Shall I be seeing you all again tomorrow?" he asked.

"Sure will George. It may take us a couple of weeks to get all the material we need. And my name's Jessica; not Miss or Young Lady; I can't stand it when people say that."

"I'll remember that in the future, Jessica; bye." And he waved as we drove off.

On the drive home, I rang Larry.

"I think we're ready to go. Jess has the Security Officer eating out of her hand; so just tell us where and when."

"It's only been two days, so let's not rush it. There is a pub in Fremantle, close to the marina, called the Anchor Hotel. Meet me there at nine this evening and we'll iron out the final details."

"Can I come too?" asked Jess.

How could I say no? It had been less than a week, but I could see how much she was pining for her love. She had been right when she had accused me of jealousy; she had found a good man in Alex, and I had never formed any relationship that lasted more than a few nights.

"Sure, why not. As long as you feel up to it."

***

Chapter 8

It was only a thirty-minute drive from Daniel's house to the Anchor Hotel. A large old timber, two storey building with most of the ground floor given over to the bar and recreation areas; darts, pool tables, and small stage where a country singer was giving it her best with a Dolly Parton rendition of 'Nine to Five.'

In the far corner sat Alex, Larry, and Dom.

"Where's Jason?" I asked as they stood up to greet us.

"Back at home looking after the shop," explained Alex, before giving Jess a hug and passionate kiss.

Larry sent Dom to the bar for the drinks, whilst we got into a huddle around the table and Larry held court.

"Ok guys, as I said earlier, we don't need to rush things. From what you have told me, Jess had the Security Officer dangling on a piece of string; let's keep it that way."

I could see the smile on Alex's face drain away.

"So, how old is this bloke?" he asked.

"Don't look so worried Alex, he's a middle-aged man. Now how can I describe him?" She paused. "I suppose he looks like George Clooney, so obviously not my type. No, there's nothing for you to worry about," she teased.

"Is that your Land Cruiser parked outside?" Larry asked us, wanting to change the subject.

"Yes, bit of an old bus, but well serviced and a good runner." I assured him.

"I'm sure it does, what size are the wheels? They need to be identical for the exchange." He then sent Dom out to jot down the tyre specs.

"There is a very quiet little cove on the north-west corner, with an off-road track leading down to the water. It could take three or four days, depending on how much we can pack into a tyre."

"What about the diamonds?" I asked.

"Let's get one job done at a time. Anyway, that's for you to sort out; go hire a boat and take your uncle out on a fishing trip, and don't forget the ice."

"Well, I'm no angler, and I'm not sure whether uncle is," I hesitantly stated.

"Don't worry Connor, Dom and Jason will supply the fish; there's a glut of Pink Snapper at the moment. I'll get a dozen put by, just bring the Eskies and ice."

We finished our drinks, and I got up to leave.

"It's still early. You go if you're ready, Alex and I will stay for a bit, and I'll get an Uber home."

It was only half nine; how could I say no?

"Ok, but don't be too late. We've an early start in the morning."

"What? An early start to do a fictitious job. Are you having a laugh?"

She was right; we were going to the island for a picnic whilst pretending to do some research. There was no urgency; we had another day to kill before we started our smuggling operation.

"I suppose you're right," I conceded. "I'm off for a good night's sleep anyway. I'll see you in the morning and don't wake the household when you come in."

Larry, Dom, and I drank up, and we left the couple smooching on the dance floor to "When you say nothing at all."

I looked back over my shoulder as the door swung closed; yes, I felt the pangs of jealousy; a loving couple on the dance floor and a gorgeous singer on the mic.

As I drove back to Daniel's house, I vowed that when this was all sorted out, I would clean up my act and find a partner of my own.

11.00am on the third day, a smartly groomed officer greeted us. George Ferguson had tidied up his appearance, a haircut and freshly pressed uniform.

As Jess opened the driver's window, his breath no longer smelt of alcohol or any other odours, only the distinct smell of aftershave.

"Good morning Jessica, you guys are a bit on the drag this morning," he politely commented.

"You know how it is George; my brother had a late one last night, and we struggled to get him out of bed this morning, so we booked the later ferry." She replied, the lying little madam!

"Well, have a good day, I expect I'll see you this afternoon." He asked with an air of expectancy.

"If there's no other way off the island, then you probably will," she joked. "By the way, I love your new aftershave; it suits you." She remarked as we drove towards the ferry, leaving the red-faced officer longing after her like a puppy dog.

On the island, we checked out the cove that Larry had suggested; it was perfect.

It was an easily negotiable off-road track leading down to the secluded bay, where we would be hidden from any road traffic.

At lunchtime we ate our pack-ups on the beach away from prying eyes and I envisaged how the exchange of wheels would take place.

If carried out correctly, should take no longer than five minutes. And with George now drooling over Jess, we should be ready for Larry to make the first drop tomorrow.

After lunch Jess and I took a dip, Daniel declined the offer to join us; his days of frolicking in the sea were long gone, happy to sit and watch us enjoying ourselves.

On our return to Fremantle, Jess had turned up the heat on the unsuspecting George and slipped on a wet tee shirt.

She got out of the driver's seat and went to open the rear door. George put on a pretence of inspecting the rear of the vehicle but could not take his eyes off her.

"Been swimming today Jessica?"

"Yes George, it was such a beautiful day; I couldn't resist a quick dip before we returned. Do you enjoy swimming?"

"Well, I never did when I lived in Scotland; the sea was like ice. But yes, I have come to love the occasional dip since I moved over here."

"You look as though you've kept yourself fit; I can just imagine you in your boardie's." She provocatively taunted.

"Well, if you're free this weekend, there are some great beaches along the coast that I can show you."

"That's an enticing thought George. Can we take a rain check? Once we have finished helping uncle, I'll have loads of free time."

"Fair enough, I'll hold you to that," he confidently smiled.

"Maybe the following weekend if you're not on duty." Jess then climbed back behind the wheel.

"Bye, drive safely." George waved as we drove away through the gates.

The next morning, I could not eat breakfast as I nervously contemplated the day ahead. Even Aunt Catherine was a little on edge and insisted that we all had something to eat before we left the house. I eventually succumbed to a slice of toast to go with my coffee.

The moment of truth was upon us; one slip, one wrong word, one silly mistake and all our plans could collapse around our ears, and the past few months would have been for nothing.

"Good Luck. Come home safely," Aunt called as we pulled off the driveway.

At Fremantle, George was still putting on the charm and hanging on Jess's every breath. We could all see that the poor man was falling in love, which made it easy for us to sail straight through unchallenged and onto the ferry.

Larry had informed us that high tide would be perfect for the drop off. At precisely 10.45am, the inflatable rounded the rocky spur and entered the cove. It took exactly ten minutes to roll our spare tyre twenty metres to the water's edge, complete the exchange, carry their stuffed tyre up the beach, bolt it to the rear of the Toyota. In the time it had taken us, Dom and Jason had guided the dinghy around the rocks and headed out towards the Dream Star.

At lunchtime, it was difficult to casually sit there eating our sandwiches, knowing that we had somewhere in excess of a million dollars bolted to the rear of the Land Cruiser; the vehicle stayed in my sight every minute that we were on the island.

The doting George spent five minutes chatting up Jess, then we were on our way; clear of Fremantle harbour and home to count the first shipment.

In the privacy of the garage, Daniel handed me the tyre levers, and I carefully eased the rubber away from the wheel rim; just enough to get my hand inside and pull out the first wad of notes.

As each handful came out, Daniel stuffed them into one of a stack of supermarket carrier bags, and Jess took them into the house. We ended up with eight bags full. I then re-inflated the tyre and joined the others in the dining room for the mammoth counting session.

"One million, one hundred and eighty thousand US Dollars," announced Daniel as he neatly placed the last bundle on the dining room table.

"We had better put it in my safe."

In the basement, tucked away behind a row of sliding shelves, was a huge safe, more like one that you would find in a bank, not in a private dwelling.

"Dare I ask what you keep in here, obviously not just the deeds to the house." I tentatively enquired.

"No, you may not; let's just say that I use it for business," and he gave me a knowing wink.

It was not any wonder that he could front up 150k for me without breaking a sweat. I'd love to know what his business was; I knew he had dealt in property, but to have a vault of that size in his basement beggared belief. So, I thought it better not to ask more questions about that topic.

"Larry thinks that three more trips should see the job done, then we have the small problem of laundering the money; any suggestions?" I asked, hoping Daniel would have a magical solution.

"Leave it with me. I've a few friends in the Casino business that might help, but you'll be saying goodbye to at least 30% of it."

These numbers were scrambling my brain. Three more similar shipments and we were talking roughly 4.5 million US. I took out my calculator and checked the exchange rate. It came to 6.150 million Australian Dollars. Less than 30% would leave us with 4.305 million.

I owed Larry 100k; Daniel 150k plus 10%. Kurt already had his; whatever Matthew had scooped up, plus his substantial bonus for the disposal of Ex-President Zimbala.

It would leave us with nearly 3.65 million between the four of us. All the team should be happy. Then there was Mike Simpson. I'd forgotten all about Mad Mike in my calculations. Well, Jess and I still had the diamonds, so I was sure he would be happy if I tossed a few in his direction.

After all deductions, Alex and Jason should walk away with more that 912k apiece. Jess and I the same, and we still had the diamonds to move and according to Google, the Star of Hopetown at 45.5 carats is estimated at somewhere over 300 million dollars.

I could not sleep that night, imagining all the things that our family could do with our reclaimed fortune.

Then the sad thoughts of my father and the urge for revenge penetrated my brain; when the time was right, someone was going to suffer.

Collecting the next shipment was a doddle, a carbon copy of the previous day.

But when we turned up on the third day, it surprised us to see that there was a different security officer.

"No George today," Jess asked as the young female officer waved us through the gate.

"No, it's his day off. Why do you have a message for him?" she helpfully enquired.

"Not a problem, I'll catch him tomorrow." And we drove onto the ferry.

My first instinct was to abort today's collection, but Jess and Daniel felt confident the young female officer seemed friendly and did not pose a problem.

We did not mention the change of security officer as we quickly swapped the tyres.

Over lunch, Daniel attempted to quell our fears.

"It will not be a problem if we keep calm, as we have all week. Relax, enjoy the lunch and the scenery."

The young officer pulled us to one side as we came off the ferry.

"I take it you're all aware of what you can and cannot take off the island."

"Yes, officer, we have been coming all week and George Ferguson made it perfectly clear. The only thing that we take away are our photos, and the only thing that we leave are our footprints." Said Jess with a smile.

"I wish everyone did the same, but do you mind if I have a look in the back?"

"Be our guest, and Jess accompanied her and opened the rear door. The keen young officer, eyeing Jess' condition, had a thorough look under the picnic blankets, examining the cameras and binoculars.

"Nice equipment," she said as Jess closed the door.

The officer then stopped and squeezed the tyre.

Jess froze in her tracks. Why had they not heeded my advice and aborted today's exchange? I jumped out of the car; I could see the look of horror on her face.

"Are you aware that your spare is flat?"

"Yes, officer, I was going to ask you where the nearest garage was. Jess picked up a nail on the off-road track; it took me nearly half an hour to change it."

"Not a problem. There's a tyre fitter nearby. Take the first left at the roundabout and it's a kilometre further up the road."

"Thank you officer, shall we be seeing you tomorrow?"

"No, I normally work in the office. George Ferguson is back on duty tomorrow."

Once we had driven through the gates, we took a collective sigh of relief. We had got away with it this time, but they would never talk me out of following my instincts again.

That was one mistake that we should not have made. Ferguson had offered to take Jess to the beach, and we had not picked up on the fact that QED; he could not be in two places at once!

Having made such a fundamental mistake, I thought it better not to mention it to the others.

The final cash collection went without a hitch.

George was back from his rostered day off. Pleased to see Jess and suck up more of her promises of a day at the beach the following weekend.

***

Chapter 9

To my surprise, uncle Daniel had been an expert angler in his day, and still had his collection of rods and tackle.

One of his friends owned a nice little six-seater tinny with outboard motor and was happy to let him take it out.

Daniel guided me as I backed down the ramp and our small craft bobbed on the water. We detached the trailer, and I parked the Toyota. Then delicately climbed aboard, in fear of tipping it over; It seemed so unstable after sailing on Larry's ninety-foot yacht.

One tug of the cord and Daniel had fired up the motor. We slowly headed away from the ramp and other boats. Fifty metres out and he cut the motors, and we drifted as he attached bait to the two lines and we fed the fish; I was useless and had little idea what I was doing, but comforted by the thought that it mattered little whether we actually caught anything, as Dom and Jason would already have done all the hard work for us.

For appearance' sake, we chugged along the coast, and caught a couple of fish, neither of which were large enough to keep, so tossed them back into the sea.

I looked at my watch; 11.30, time to venture into deeper waters for our meeting with Larry and the boys.

Alex jumped down to help me lift the two Eskies aboard the yacht. I scattered the uncut diamonds until they had all sunk to the bottom of the ice; from the top you would never have been able to differentiate between the stones and the ice. Then the dozen good sized snapper, all freshly caught an hour earlier.

Finally, I opened the small casket that contained the 'Star of Hopetown' and carefully placed it in the bottom corner of the second Eskie; If the others knew the value of that stone, I would probably have a mutiny on my hands: Thankfully they did not, and I was not about to enlighten them on the subject!

We lowered the two ice boxes back into the tinny.

Jason pushed us away from the yacht, and Daniel restarted the motor.

The calm water of the morning changed, and a strong breeze whipped up the waves as we headed inland.

I had survived the storms in the Indian Ocean but would not fancy our chances in the open top bucket that we were bobbing around in, and we were making little progress in reaching the shore.

Then from behind us came a loud blast of a siren; it was a vessel from the Fisheries Authority. It pulled alongside and an officer climbed down to join us.

"What the hell are you two doing this far out in this tin bath? Are you mad?"

"Sorry officer, we got carried away; the Snapper were biting like crazy; I've never caught so many. In all the excitement, we just went out further than we should; we didn't know that the weather was about to change,"

"Snapper. Ok, show me what got you so excited," he insisted.

I proudly opened the lids of both ice boxes to display our catch.

"Fair enough, and they all look a good size to be keepers; I don't really blame you, but in future stay closer to the shoreline, or buy yourselves a bigger more seaworthy boat." With that said, he climbed back aboard his vessel.

"Cop hold of this," and he threw us a line. "We'll tow you back into the calmer waters,"

I thanked him and prayed to God that this would be my last adventure at sea, aboard a tinny, yacht or any other type of boat!

In the seclusion of the garage, Daniel and I opened the lids of the boxes, removed the fish and with Catherine's hair dryer melted away the ice, leaving the watery treasure at the bottom.

I dipped my hand into the corners and felt for the rock.

Catherine gasped as I opened my dripping hand to reveal the Star of Hopetown.

"Wow, it looks much larger than in the photos that I'd seen." Tears of emotion running down her face. "Your father would be so proud of you."

"Yes Aunt; our fortune has come home," and I handed her the diamond before we scooped out the rest of the stones and placed them onto a towel to dry, separating the cut from the uncut ones.

Daniel counted them and carefully wrapped each one into a piece of tissue: Fourteen cut and two hundred and eighty uncut diamonds; we placed them on three trays, and they were locked away in the vault with all the cash.

"I'm no expert, but the stones have got to be worth several millions, so what do you plan to do with them?" asked Daniel as he poured the drinks.

"I was thinking it should be a four-way split; Aunty Catherine, mother, Jess and me. We would have been the ones to inherit the Mine, had we not been shafted by the government over there."

"But how can we divide the Star?" asked Aunt, as she sat in her armchair, still clutching the diamond.

"Well Aunt, we only have two choices; we either auction it or keep it as a family heirloom."

"That's something that we will all have to give serious thought to; in the meantime, it needs to be safely locked away in the vault," Daniel insisted.

He was right; there was no need to rush into anything and it had to be a cordial agreement between all concerned.

The thought of auctioning the Star had its appeal; however in proving its provenance and our current ownership, would risk laying a trail that might lead the assassination of Ex-President Zimbala to our doorstep; Yes, it was an option that needed serious thought!

If it was to be passed down the family line, it should go to Aunty; after her it would be Jess, then her offspring; or mine should I ever produce one.

It was a conundrum that would have to wait until the morning; now it was the time for celebrations, so maybe another glass of bubbles before we went to bed.

We spent the next morning locked in Daniel's study.

He was confident that his friends at the Casino could launder the cash; although it would not be done overnight; it might take several months.

As far as the diamonds were concerned, he liked the idea of keeping the Star in the family. He had no connections in the jewellery trade, so moving the other uncut stones would be down to me and Jess.

At twelve noon, we collected Jason and Alex from the Anchor; I settled my account with Larry; said our goodbyes and drove back to Daniel's in the old Toyota.

We discussed our return to Queensland. There was no way we could get through customs with bags full of uncut diamonds, so flying was out of the question. It would be another road trek, but with the four of us sharing the driving and barring accidents, we could complete the journey in one go.

We had crossed the width of the Continent twice before, but this time we could afford to travel in comfort, so that afternoon we purchased the latest Toyota Land Cruiser 300 series 4x4 SUV.

The Sales assistant nearly choked when I pulled out a wad and placed the $150,000 into his sweaty palm.

Our last evening in Perth, and again Daniel insisted on taking us to the poshest restaurant in the city. He said we needed to adapt to our new lifestyle of wining and dining in the best places now that we were all wealthy citizens.

Before leaving in the morning, Daniel took our bank details, and promised to keep us all afloat while he sorted the finances from his end. He would keep the Star safe until we came to a consensus of what we should do; he was sure that our mother would like to have a say as it would have gone to my father had nature have taken its course.

Aunt Catherine and Daniel stood waving as I took the first stint at the wheel of our new car and we headed back to Queensland, to reunite with mother and Patrick.

***

Book 4: Sweet Revenge.

Chapter 1

We had agreed that a two-hour spell at the wheel would be the most efficient plan; pausing only for a quick pit stop and snack on the changeovers.

After our previous uncomfortable journey in Patrick's old wagon, Jess and I were enjoying the luxury of the brand-new vehicle. It felt as though we were floating on air, cruising along in our top of the range SUV.

We sped along the Eyre Highway into South Australia, then north along the Outback Highway and through the Ranges. Halfway into our 40-hour journey, and the terrain was changing; more inclines, twists, and turns; the Toyota was being put through its paces and responding well to the challenge, as we tried to keep up with our time schedule.

The last time I had arrived in Burgville, was in Jessica's old Beetle, but this time we arrived at the Clover Sheep Station in style, although it might not have appeared that way to mother and Patrick, as we pulled up in our dirt covered Toyota.

Hugs, kisses, and introductions were made.

Jess proudly introducing Alex as her fiancé; holding back the revelation regarding the baby until we were all sat at the dining table.

We had been gone for months and mother wanted to know every last detail; most of which was revealed, although I held back on the gruesome accounts about Mozambique.

Charlie and Keon had been invited to join in our celebrations. Both were keen to hear all the details of the adventure, though really disappointed that they had not been a part of it.

Then they both went quiet; left the room and sat out on the veranda.

After twenty minutes, they had not returned, so I went out to see where they were. They both sat smoking and whispering.

"What's up guys?" I asked as I handed them a beer.

"Nothing; we're really pleased for you, but." Charlie took a swig, then sadly looked down at his feet.

"But what Charlie? We are supposed to be friends, so cough it up; what's eating you?"

"Ok Connor, we're both pleased for you and the family; but where does that leave us?" and he voiced his concerns. "You have all made your fortunes and will probably sell up and leave the territory; I would if I were you. I'd head for the coast and the highlife."

"We're not blaming you, man, but what happens to us now? No job, no accommodation; how do we survive? There are no farms for miles and none that need any extra hands." Keon joined in; he too was concerned.

"Drink your beer and stop worrying. I've just had a forty-hour drive; that's a lot of thinking time. I have a few ideas that will wait until the morning, so for now come inside and join the party. I promise you we will see you right; and more!"

We returned to the dining room, just as mother and Jess emerged from the kitchen.

"Quiet everyone, I have one more important announcement to make. I've already told mother, and now want everyone to know. Alex and I are expecting a baby."

This proclamation prompted another round of drinking which continued until the early hours.

The following morning, all Patrick's plans to move the herd of cattle went out of the window. Except for Jess and mother, we were waking with thick heads from the previous night; the past weeks we'd had to abstain from the booze; our bodies were out of practice, even Jason looked like 'death warmed up.' This was not the time to discuss my master plan, although I needed to speak to mother.

Mid-morning we sat on the deck, sipping yet another cup of coffee, and I broached the subject of father's death, the accident and lack of compensation.

As teenage children, we had not been given all the details. All I remember was that father had a well-paid job as a mining engineer, a fly-in fly- out worker to a mine somewhere in central Queensland.

The accident had brought our world crashing down; we were broke and we eventually moved, exchanging our friends and beautiful home in Brisbane, for the run-down farm that Patrick owned.

"I'm not blaming Patrick; quite the opposite. The man has been a saint. But I really need to know what actually caused that low point in our lives. Why was there no compensation? Why did we have to move?"

Mother's sad eyes welled up as the distant memories returned. Was I being cruel? Yes, possibly; but this time I needed to know everything.

"Your father worked for the Australasia Mining Corporation, owned by Colin Handley, the multi-millionaire mining magnate; a ruthless bastard who has shares in virtually every mine in the country; gold, diamond, copper, or coal. His smarmy persona that you see on the television does not match the black heart of the man; a big fat jovial character, always promising the earth to his employees, whilst shafting them at the same time, if you'll excuse the puns. The only earth that the men in the Glendale Mining disaster got, was the mud that buried them."

What had I done? My mother, the quiet little stay-at-home parent and bookworm, was letting out her years of frustration and pent-up anger; I had never seen her so animated; fists clenched and a red flushed face, looking about to burst.

"After the accident he appeared on the television; full of sympathy for the families and promising that the company would look after them all; the families received a pittance in compensation, just enough to keep them from starving. We took out a 'Class Action' against him, but after waiting two years for it to come to court, the Judge weighed in his favour; He was obviously one of Handley's old pals, so we ended up with bugger all, other than the solicitor's bills."

By now I was also swelling with anger; if I ever wanted vengeance for my father's death, then Colin Handley was my target!

"So tell me mother, exactly how much revenge would you like me to inflict?" I asked as I sat holding her hand.

***

Chapter 2

After lunch, everyone was feeling a little more compos mentis from last night's partying, so I called them together and outlined my plans.

"The four of us have the best part of a million each, but all that mother and Patrick have is a farm that was losing money year after year. Sorry Pat, I don't mean to sound cruel; you know it's true. In reality, all that we have here is a worthless acreage of scrubland."

"You ungrateful little …" he jumped up and was about to protest, mother grabbed his arm.

"Wait and listen to what Connor has to say."

Patrick reluctantly sat back down.

"Hear me out Pat; and I'll explain how we'll turn this farm into a gold mine. Well, a diamond mine, to be exact," I corrected myself with a cunning grin. "You have shared all that you have with Jess and me, so it should go without saying that what we have is yours."

He relaxed back into his seat, but his face had turned a deep shade of red.

"Besides the Cash, the Star of Hopetown, and the other cut diamonds, we also have the two hundred and eighty uncut stones. Yes, I can see what you are all thinking; cut or uncut, they are still diamonds and worth a fortune to be shared amongst family and friends." I could see their eyes light up at the thought of another substantial payout.

"Sadly not! My plan for these is to create a diamond mine on our worthless piece of dirt, then sell it to a certain gentleman who goes by the name of Colin Handley."

"What!" exclaimed Alex; "Handley the multimillionaire."

"The very same." I then related the story that mother had told me earlier. They all listened intently; not one question or interruption.

"You can all see how important this is; my father should have been the one to inherit the fortune, along with mother, who had not only been denied any share of the inheritance, then received no real compensation after the mining disaster, along with the other eleven families. I intend to ensure that everyone gets their just deserts; including Colin Handley."

I looked around the room and studied their faces; were they in or out?

"Does my suggestion have your approval?" I asked.

Each in turn smiled, and they gave a collective reply.

"Yes."

"Thanks for your support. We'll meet again tomorrow morning to draw up the finer details. Now, does anyone fancy a beer?"

In the morning, it was time to reveal my grand plan for the discovery of diamonds in central Queensland.

Sheep Station Creek had run through the land for hundreds of years, although for the last three it had been nothing other than a dry bed of red sand.

This had been the main reason for the struggles that faced Patrick, who was constantly moving the cattle in search of water and greener pastures.

I recalled the story in Aunt Catherine's book, of how a small child discovered a shiny stone, which eventually resulted in the Diamond Rush all those years ago in Africa. I planned to replicate the discovery here in Australia, using two of Charlie's and Keon's nephews.

A week later, I invited them to the farm for a BBQ and an impromptu game of cricket. It was a good gathering; twenty or thirty of us; mother, Patrick, and our group, plus two dozen of Charlie's brothers, sisters, friends, and their children.

Alex delighted in the manly task of barbequing the spit roast pig, beef steaks and snags, whilst Jessica, his attentive fiancée, prepared and served out the salads and Jason had the responsibility of keeping the beers cold.

When everyone had been fed, it was time for the game.

The flattest area to set up the wicket was on the dried-out creek bed; we set up the stumps, from broken tree branches.
The bat and ball, were the ones I had played with at school many years earlier; we were ready, and the game started.

Twenty minutes into the game I noticed that two of the younger children had lost interest and had taken to hitting stones with sticks; a perfect time for the discovery.

I walked past the two boys and discreetly dropped a small handful of uncut stones, then gave Charlie the nod and walked away, distancing myself from the playing children.

It only took a few minutes until their improvised game progressed to the shiny round stones.

"Uncle Charlie, look at these ones," the elder of the two called.

Charlie took a stone and gave it a good rub, then called us over.

"What do you think guys?" and he handed it around the group that had abandoned the game and gathered around to see what was occurring.

"Well, I'm no expert, but it looks like a diamond," said Charlie's sister, who had given it another rub and held it up to the light.

"Are there any more?" asked mother.

And they excitedly started scrabbling around on their hands and knees. I held back and watched as our unsuspecting witnesses discovered another half a dozen shiny stones.

They handed seven stones the size of small marbles to mother; everyone eagerly pushing forward, wanting to see and touch the diamonds. All in the belief that the dried-up river bed had thrown up this fantastic treasure; Mother and Patrick had struck it lucky, and a fortune lay ahead, and this was just the start!

It was getting late into the afternoon, and the sun was disappearing beyond the distant mountains.

Most of the food had been eaten. Mother and Jess packed anything left as takeaways for our departing guests. They said their goodbyes and headed for home in their selection of trucks and Utes.

We sat on the deck and watched, as the last of them disappeared into the twilight.

Phase one of my plan had gone well. I knew that once they had returned to the small town, the news of our diamonds would spread like wildfire; tomorrow was going to be a very busy day.

The next morning was quiet. I stood on the deck looking the length of our track that leads off the main road, expecting to see masses of reporters descending upon us; but no, not a soul.

Both Charlie and Keon had gone home with their families and had been given the day off, so there was no one to ask what was happening in town.

At eleven o'clock, my impatience got the better of me.

"Get changed Jess, we're going into town."

"What for, brother? Be patient, it's a case of let Mohamed come to the mountain, not the other way around. What was a good plan yesterday is still a good plan today!"

Jess was soon proved right.

I waited until noon then could put it off no longer; picked up my phone and rang Charlie.

"What's happening bro? I've been waiting all morning and there's not a reporter in sight."

"Well, there soon will be. I put the word about like you told me, and little Birrani has become a celebrity. The local press are all over him, and wanting to come out to the farm for photos and interviews with your mob."

"Good work mate, I'll see you later," I thanked him, although I had expected more. Local press? That's hardly going to get Handley's attention.

Mother made the coffee and we all sat around the kitchen table.

"Don't look so down Connor, patience was never your strong suit. Drink your coffee; we all trust you, it will work out, just you wait and see."

I forced a smile and finished my drink. They had put their faith in me. We had come so far since I left Brisbane and returned to the family farm, yet the thoughts of revenge upon Handley were constantly playing games in my head.

Was this one dream too many; would the greedy bastard actually fall for my plan or was I wasting my time?

Two o'clock and we were disturbed by the sound of two helicopters circling overhead. I could see the emblem on the sides; it was reporters from both Seven and Nine News.

Before they landed on the empty paddock, I could see more clouds of dust, this time coming from a convoy of other vehicles headed down our track from the main road.

More journalists: suddenly my confidence had returned, and I gathered the family on to the veranda for the onslaught of reporters.

Charlie waved to us as he stepped out of a limousine with his sister and the young Birrani, having been chauffeured by a reporter from the 'Daily Australian.'

Flashing cameras and microphones being thrust at us from all directions, the two rival television news reporters jostling for the best spot to set up their equipment; it was mayhem!

I raised my voice above the noise, to gain their attention.

"Ladies and Gentlemen. Please, Ladies and Gentlemen," I implored. "Can we have some order for God's sake. We'll take questions, but only one at a time. Thank you."

Reginald Forbes from the local Gazette, a small paper with a circulation of only two or three hundred, held the advantage over all the 'Big Boys', as he was a personal friend of Patrick and mother.

"Patrick, could you tell us about this discovery? Will you be selling up, or opening your own mine?"

"Why Reg, are you about to make me an offer?" Pat replied but could not keep a straight face; all this attention and excitement, he lapsed back into his broad Irish brogue for the amusement of his old friend.

"I might Patrick, how much are you asking?"

This brought a chuckle from the others, who had turned up in a carnival atmosphere. This was the most exciting news they had to report upon for several years. Although COVID was a distant memory, the drought, the fires, and floods continued to consume their reporting.

Mother and Patrick stood with Birrani between them, and he recounted how the small boy had been playing with the shiny stones, totally unaware of what he had found.

It was on the dried bed of the creek that had not seen a flow of water in the last three years. The stones might have been washed down from the mountains at any time over a few million years. So how many more still lay there? Only time will tell.

"So the serious answer to your question, Reggie, is that we are going nowhere. This find could bring prosperity to the entire area, and employment for many."

"But do you have the financial assets to exploit your land?"

A serious question from the Channel Seven reporter.

"I guess that depends on what else we find and, of course, the findings of the geological reports. Now, all we have is a handful of uncut diamonds; nothing more."

Patrick was doing a great job of sticking to the script; we needed to keep the festival vibes going, and let our plans slowly unfold.

The circus then moved to the area of the creek bed, where Birrani re-enacted the events for the cameras and mother displayed the seven stones, neatly on a tray for the world to see.

The bait was laid, but would the Big Fish bite?

***

Chapter 3

The Geologist was a Professor Leanna Pettersen from the University of Queensland, who was accompanied by three of her third-year students.

They arrived two days after the journalists had left and pulled up in a battered old Land Rover towing a trailer with their tents and equipment.

"Welcome to the Clover Sheep Station," and I held out my hand.

We had spoken on the phone, but when she had stepped out of the driver's door, it was not the image that I had conjured up. She was no batty old professor, but an attractive middle-aged woman in designer jeans and shirt, looking as though she had just stepped off the set of an Indiana Jones movie.

I cannot deny it. My heart instantly leapt as we shook hands and I looked into her deep blue eyes; her long blonde hair tied back in a ponytail, revealing a long slender neck; skin smooth and unlined, she had instantly bewitched me.

"You can let go now, mister van Vuuren," she said with a smile.

I guess she was used to men drooling over her; and embarrassingly, I'd been no exception.

I reluctantly released her hand and offered to help with their bags and as I glanced over my shoulder I saw Alex and Jess standing on the veranda, observing our new arrivals. Jess grinning like the Cheshire Cat; there was no doubt that I would be in for some piss taking later from my dear sister!

They set up their tents at the rear of the house, next to Charlie and Keon's quarters, with access to the shower and toilet. It was an efficient operation carried out by the group of all female students who had obviously done it before; anyone in my old regiment would have been proud of them.

By now it was mid-afternoon, and mother insisted that they all came inside for a bite to eat after their long journey.

The first question from the Professor, was to enquire if Patrick O'Brien was around; she had a stack of forms she needed him to sign before she could start her work.

Mother informed her that Patrick was away for two days with Charlie, Keon and Jason rounding up the cattle. He had found a buyer, who had made an offer for the entire stock.

"I take it from that, you are confident of us finding more diamonds. Or are you just moving out of the cattle business? I know it's been hard over the past three years of drought."

"You are not wrong. These are hard times, but if it only turns out to be another few handfuls of stones, it will be enough for us to pack up and leave." Mother replied, then added, "It all depends on what you find; if anything at all."

"Well, if you can sign these forms for your husband, we'll get started straight away."

I had silently sat at the table, mesmerised by the professor. She was not only intelligent and enthusiastic, but the most captivating woman that I'd ever met.

Her students had devoured the snacks that mother had prepared and were also itching to get started.

"Ok Connor, can you show us where the diamonds were found? Then we can make a start." She asked as she stood from the table.

"Sure, anytime you're ready professor."

"It's Leanna, not professor; I'm not in the classroom now." And gave me an encouraging smile.

Leanna Pettersen; what a perfect name to suit her Scandinavian appearance, or Leanna van Vuuren? That would fit nicely too. Passionate thoughts racing away in my head; was this Goddess real or an apparition?

I led them out to where the game of cricket had taken place, and where Birrani had unwittingly made the discovery. I did not take them to where I had made my other deposits further along the dried-up river bed; those discoveries had to be made by her and the students.

Their initial search revealed nothing. The light was fading; they would resume in the morning.

It was a warm night, and I could not sleep. I lay in the silence of my room without having to suffer the perpetual snoring from Jason, I tossed and turned, unable to settle, knowing that she was only fifty metres away.

The frustration was building up in me, as I imagined her body entwined in mine. She was driving me crazy. I could see by her smile that she felt the same. I sat on the edge of my bed; I would go to her.

I dressed, then came to my senses. How could I possibly do that with the students in adjoining tents; it would cause a scandal at the university.

Get back into bed, you idiot!

I buried myself under the bedding; the torment continuing until the first light of day.

Mother had prepared a breakfast for all our visitors, and I was the last to drag myself to the table.

"You look like shit, brother. Didn't you get any sleep?"

"No, it was a sultry night, and I had a lot on my mind. Anyway, how did you campers get on?" I asked, to divert the conversation away from me.

"Fine. No strange noises and no snakes," replied Leanna.

"So, what are your plans for today?"

"Well, it will be a hands and knees day, as we work our way along the creek bed. Depending on what we find, we might make a few preliminary digs tomorrow. It could all take a few weeks, before I can submit any kind of report."

A few weeks? Great, plenty of time for me to win her over. I knew I needed to smarten up my appearance, but when all said and done, I would be one of the richest men in Australia, so how could she refuse me?

***

Chapter 4

The next few weeks passed by.

The students continued to find the odd cluster of diamonds; Leanna sent several samples of earth back to the university for analysis. Patrick had received a good price for the cattle, and they had all been transported.

All was good in the world, other than my failed attempts to win over my princess. She was always warm and friendly, but resisted any of my clumsy attempts to draw her into an intimate situation. She had disclosed that she had once been married, her ex-husband lived in Sweden, so why didn't she want me?

My disappointments escalated when she handed me her preliminary report.

All the diamonds were of outstanding quality and would be worth a considerable sum. Undoubtably, over time, more would be found. At this point there was no evidence of where the source might be. Her team had taken samples over a distance of five kilometres and found nothing to suggest that there was sufficient evidence to recommend mining the area.

"Are you sure? They haven't just fallen from the sky; It must be worth setting up a mine; surely," I pressed her.

She gave me a sympathetic look.
"I'm sorry, Connor, I can only report on what I have found; I would be lying if I did otherwise. You could still go ahead with the mining,

who knows what you may find, but you might throw away all that you have found in a fool's dream of success. My advice to you, would be to take what you have found and enjoy it."

It wasn't her advice that I wanted; it was a report proclaiming that there was a potential fortune laying under the dirt on our farm.

I was really going off the bitch; she had rejected all my advances and had now kicked me in the balls again by offering up this pathetic report; The patronising cow!

I bit my tongue and offered an unconvincing smile.

"Oh well, I guess you are right Leanna, what we have must be worth at least a million, so I must not get greedy."

"That's the spirit Connor; a bird in the hand and all that."

After dinner that evening, I helped myself to one of Patrick's bottles of Irish Whisky; it had been a long while since I had indulged myself in a proper drink.

Leanne and her girls had retired to their tents, Patrick, Alex, Jess and Jason had driven into town for the evening. Mother had taken a good book to bed, so I sat alone drinking in the dark and reflected upon the events of the past few weeks.

What I had thought was a brilliant plan to make our fortune and at the same time wreak revenge on that swine Colin Handley had disappeared into dust.

My desires and fantasies about the beautiful Leanna, had left me whimpering like a wounded dog. What was wrong with me? What had suddenly made me so repulsive in the woman's eyes? Questions that I could not answer.

I was halfway down the bottle when I decided to have it out with her. They were planning to leave in the morning, but before she packed up and left, I had to know what she thought was wrong with me.

I drained the glass and stormed out to the tents.

As I approached, I could hear a muffled giggling coming from her tent. I paused, then tiptoed closer. The laughter turning into urgent spasms of grunts. I crawled closer on my hands and knees, then peered under the tent flap.

To my astonishment, they were all naked and Leanna on her back, being pleasured by her students.

They were so engaged in their love making; touching, caressing, and kissing, that they were oblivious to the eyes of the watcher. Then the gasp and look of horror as she realised that they were playing to an audience of one.

I didn't know who was the more horrified; her or me!

She sat upright, reached for the sheet to cover her breasts, then screamed.

"Get out, you pervert. Get out!" she yelled.

The other three girls turned to face me, so I instantly pulled my head back, dragged myself to my feet and drunkenly scrambled and stumbled my way back to the house; another drink was desperately needed.

The sight of her naked body had driven a stake through my heart; the woman I lusted after giving herself to the young girls.

I sat in the darkness, tears running down my cheeks. Over the past few weeks, I had raised my levels of expectancy on all fronts, which had turned into an unmitigated disaster. My fortune, revenge, and romance had been cruelly torn away from me.

I took the bottle to my room, swigged down the remains, and fell onto the bed in a drunken stupor.

I awoke the next morning. Jason snoring in the bed opposite; I had not heard them when they had returned. I doubted that the pipes and drums of the Scottish Royal Highlanders would have woken me that night.

I rubbed my eyes and my sore head. Through the mist and buzzing in my ears, I could hear the clatter of the girls outside, packing their tents and loading the trailer.

Leanna saw me watching her from my window, her face reddened, and she waved to me to come outside.

She took me by the arm and led us to the privacy of the barn.

"About last night," she paused and checked that no one was in ear shot. "About last night, I can explain."

"I don't think that it needs any explanation, I know I was pissed, but I'm not blind."

"Don't be like that Connor, it was our last night and we'd had a few drinks; it just got out of hand. I promise you it was a drunken one off. Nothing more. If the university found out, it would cost me my job. I can trust you to keep it quiet, can't I Connor?" she pleaded.

What trust me, she must be mad! But she might buy my silence at a price. Suddenly my plans for revenge on Colin Handley had been resurrected.

"Of course, you can trust me Leanna, I would never drop a friend in the shit; and we are friends, aren't we?"

"Sure, we are friends; I'd do the same for you if the roles were different." She replied, having regained her confidence.

"That's good to hear," and my serious face lightened to a cunning smile. "Now, about this report that you are going to write."

***

Chapter 5

We waved as the Land Rover and trailer disappeared in a cloud of dust, having completed the surveying, and compiled their reports.

Would Professor Leanna Pettersen keep her word? We knew she was scheduled to make a press release the following morning; all we could do was wait and keep our fingers crossed.

The next morning, we all huddled around the television to catch the early morning news. We kept channel hopping, but there were no reports concerning the diamond find. The initial find had caused a stir, but I guess it was now old news.

Surely Leanna hadn't bottled out. Maybe she thought I would never go through with my veiled threats to expose her nocturnal activities.

She was probably right. What would all my mates think? I'd look a prize prick; a jealous admirer who had told tales out of spite, just to get the woman sacked.

Then, Channel Seven News did one of their promos, where the show's presenter chats to the presenter of the next program, letting out a spoiler or two.

"In our lunchtime edition we discover whether there are diamonds in Queensland, when we interview Professor Leanna Pettersen from the university, who has spent the last few weeks trying to discover the source of the diamonds."

"That sounds great. I'm sure all our viewers will tune in, then getting out their shovels and spades ready for the Great Diamond Stampede."

I was not sure about all their viewers, but I knew we would certainly be tuning in.

We spent the next two hours kicking about with nothing to do, on a Sheep Station that had no sheep. The last of the cattle had been collected days earlier. All that was left were the six horses in the paddock, and acres upon acres of barren land.

Yes, we had a substantial fortune in both cash and diamonds, still I lusted for more, not just wealth, I really wanted revenge; would I get it? It all rested upon what Leanna said on the lunchtime news.

Twelve o'clock and we were again gathered around the television.

The Professor stood on the lawn of the university; looking as beautiful as she did on the day she first stepped out of the Land Rover at the Clover Sheep Station; and despite all that I knew, she still set my heart pounding.

"Professor Pettersen, please answer the question that all Queenslanders are asking. Are there diamonds in Queensland or not?" the reporter held out the microphone in front of her.

"Well, as the owner of the land informed me, they didn't fall out of the sky," she quipped with a pleasant smile. "But seriously, my team has spent several weeks and made a thorough exploration of the dried-up riverbed. We discovered many other pockets of diamonds that, at some time in history, have been washed down the river. I know in my mind that when Mr Patrick O'Brien, the owner of the land, invests in a diamond mine, it will be one of the greatest in the history of Australia."

"So, when will this all happen?" the reporter eagerly asked.

"I'm sure Mr O'Brien may want a second opinion before he starts this monumental undertaking, and I would not blame him for that, but as an experienced geologist, I can assure him he is onto a winner."

"Thank you, professor." And he turned to camera. "Well, there you have it, a diamond mine in Central Queensland and you heard it here first on Seven News. Now back to the Studio."

Leanna had done it; we were back on track.

"So what now asked mother?" as she switched off the set.

"We sit and wait again." This was becoming a game of patience, and only a cool head would win the match.

By the end of the day, we had been inundated with phone calls; Channel Seven and others, wanting to send reporters for interviews and photo shoots. Mother and Patrick had now become minor celebrities and were enjoying every minute of it.

Little Birrani and his mother had moved into the quarters with Charlie and Keon. All of them loving the limelight, particularly the men who were being paid as stockmen, on a farm with no stock.

The reporters had collected their photos, interviews and moved on to other news items.

"What now?" mother asked her stock question and received my usual response.

"We sit and wait."

"Wait for what, for God's sake."

Mother was getting bored; the lively atmosphere, the coming and going of the reporters, the questions and attention from the media. She had never known the like; but this week the hubbub had been replaced by a houseful of people getting under her feet. None of us had a job to go to, all of us kicking around and waiting.

A week later it happened; there would be no more waiting.

It was midmorning.

A large black helicopter with gold embossed insignia on its side that read "Australasia Mining Corporation " landed on the empty front paddock and we all gathered along the veranda to watch the spectacle.

As the dust settled, we could make out the large rotund figure of Colin Handley as he emerged down the steps and headed towards us. Two men flanked him; his associates, but associates in what? they never spoke and looked more like bodyguards than business people and by the cut of their jackets I was almost certain that they were carrying a weapon; probably automatic pistols.

"G'day. Which one of you mob is Paddy O'Brien?" he abruptly called up to us as they approached the foot of the stairs.

Handley was a man of huge proportions, now in his mid-sixties and a barrel of lard. He had been an athlete in his youth, but no longer. No neck, a shiny bald head, his clean-shaven face carried an inane smile of total insincerity; the sort of fat face that anyone would love to punch.

I had been told that he was not a man to be trusted, and from what I knew about him already, it would take some convincing to make me think otherwise.

"And what can we be doing for you on this fine day?" Patrick asked as he touched the peak of his hat in a small gesture of acknowledgement.

"Are you the Paddy that lives on this piece of dirt?"

"If you mean the Clover Sheep Station, then yes sir, that would be me. And who is it that would be asking?"

We loved it when Patrick put on the Irish brogue; kept his cool and pretended to be the half-wit.

There was no invitation up to the house. He was happy to hold the high ground and talk down to the man; determined not to be intimidated by the fat ogre.

"You know full well who I am. Don't see any sheep or other beasts apart from a few scrawny looking horses in the other paddock, so I'll asked you again, is this scrubland yours?"

"And if you listened carefully, you would have heard my first answer. Yes, I am, but what business is it of yours?" a cheeky reply, to which we all struggled to suppress our amusement.

"Cut the blarney Paddy, you know why I'm here; so how much?" Handley's face turned a deep purple; he was not enjoying the encounter with the little Irishman.

"Depends how much you'd be wanting to pay sir; make me an offer."

Patrick was playing a blinder, and we could see that Handley was struggling to keep his cool.

"I'm a busy man and don't have time to piss about. One million; take it or leave it."

"That's a very generous offer, Mr Handley; one million an acre, now that is very generous of you."

"Don't be clever with me my Mick friend, you're not back in Paddyland trading horses, you know exactly what I mean."

The veins were sticking out in Handley's neck. I thought that he was about to explode.

"Indeed, I do, sir. So, it would only be fair to let you know that I have Mr Wong and his consortium coming to see me tomorrow. They have put in an opening bid of ten million. Of course, I would prefer to sell to an Australian, but you know how it is when your horse trading."

Handley was not amused.

"Chinese consortium, what a load of bollocks. But ok, I'll match their offer, if you can prove that they actually exist. I'll call back in a few days, when you've had time to consider my offer; it will be my final one, so think very carefully before you do anything stupid Paddy."

With that, he turned and marched back to the helicopter, with his two henchmen at his side. There was another dust storm as they took off, and we returned indoors for a family conference.

We were all over Patrick for the confident way in which he had dealt with Handley. Though once inside, his hands were shaking as he attempted to pour himself a whiskey.

"Let me do that." Jess took both bottle and glass, then poured the drink. "Anyone else?" she enquired before replacing the screw cap.

"You do realise that it's only eleven o'clock husband," mother called in rebuke; then relented and gave him a kiss on the cheek. "Enjoy it Pat, you deserve one after that performance."

We were all in high spirits. The meeting with Handley had gone much as expected. However, I had two nagging concerns I needed to share with Alex and Jason, so the three of us took a stroll around the paddock.

"Handley's business associates; the taller of the two who had stood to his right; I know him from somewhere but cannot place him. Did either of you recognise him?"

"Looked a bit like Buchanan, server on our first tour."

"Yes, that's right Alex, it's coming back to me. Davy Buchanan, an absolute psycho who got kicked out of the regiment after his first tour in Afghanistan. I never really knew the guy, only by his reputation and the nasty rumours that were going around."

"Thanks Jason, I know who you're talking about, and that probably answers my other concern."

"Which is?" asked Alex.

"I didn't like Handley's parting comment; *'Think very carefully before you do anything stupid Paddy.'* It sounded very much like a shrouded threat to me." I explained.

"Handley didn't make his fortune by being nice to people; he's in a tough industry where they don't all play by the rules. I certainly would put nothing past him, so we should be prepared for a rough ride," warned Jason.

The three of us shared the same concerns, but to what degree should we involve the others? We solved this conundrum when we returned to the house.

Jess, mother, and Patrick were sat at the kitchen table; their earlier mood of excitement replaced by three serious looking faces; they had also realised that Handley's passing shot was a threat.

It was past midday and mother busied herself making lunch.

"So where do we go from here?" asked Jess as we started on the pile of sandwiches.

"We have to play it straight with Handley; at least to start with." I suggested. Ten million is not a bad offer. After all, he'd only be buying a pile of dirt, which in all honesty we would have been happy to accept half a million from anyone a few months ago."

"Yes, but there is no Chinese Consortium, so the ten million is just pie in the sky," stated the now despondent Patrick; his impromptu creation of the fictitious Mr Wong had come back to haunt him.

Then Jess came up with an idea.

"Of course, there is a Consortium of Chinese." She said with a grin.

"What are you on about?" asked mother; "Have you been at the whiskey too?"

"No. I'm as sober as a judge." She grinned, then put forward her idea.

She had a friend in Longridge, whose parents owned the Chinese restaurant on the high street. All we needed was a small group of Asians, suited up like business people, loads of photos around the farm, all smiles, and handshakes. Then put it out on Facebook that a deal had been struck for them to buy the land and mine for diamonds.

"I love it!" I exclaimed. "Sister, you're a bloody marvel!"

***

Chapter 6

Two days later, the plan had been enacted; I thanked them and paid the six players a thousand dollars each.

The news spread like wildfire, and a day later I received a phone call, not from Handley, but from Davy Buchanan.

"How can I help you, Davy?" I innocently asked.

"You know full well van Vuuren; Mr H is fucking fuming, so you'd better tell your Paddy friend to call off any deal with the chinks, or anyone else. My boss offered him a good price, so don't piss about or there will be repercussions; and I'm sure you understand what I mean by that."

"Ok Davy, don't get overexcited; there's no need for us to go to war over this. Look, I don't wish to piss anyone off, but if we sideline the Chinese with no explanation, we'll end up with their government on everyone's backs. I'm sure Mr Handley wouldn't want that either. However, if he were to double the offer, I'm sure we could change horses with no loss of face to our Chinese friends."

"What, twenty million; are you having a laugh?"

"Ok, maybe not twenty; but it has to be substantially more than what the Chinese have offered. Fifteen would be enough to let them walk away, causing no trouble."

"I'll speak to Handley; as I said, he is not a happy man, so don't hold your breath." And he ended the call.

The others had been gathered around and listened to the conversation with Buchanan.

"Do you think Handley will buy it?" asked Patrick.

"I think so; we put him into a race against the Chinese and he's a man that hates to lose. Also, the thoughts of owning the largest diamond mine in Australia appeals to his vanity. So yes, I'm sure he'll take the bait."

And so, he did.

A week later, we received a letter from Bryce, Burton, and Associates Solicitors for the Australasia Mining Corporation.

They formally made an offer for the lands and all mineral rights to the Clover Sheep Station. The property of Patrick Eugen Finbarr O'Brien.

The sum offered: $15,000,000.

"Well Patrick, do you think that you and mother will be able to survive on that," I teased as I handed the letter back to him.

"We might, provided that your mother doesn't spend it all. Seriously though, I don't know how we would have got through another year without this. Anyway, it's not all mine; the four of you deserve your share and I have Charlie and Keon to look after. Then it's off to a nice little cottage by the sea, where I can potter in the garden and your mother can sit and read to her heart's content."

That sounded perfect, and there were hugs and kisses.

My job was still only half completed. I wanted to see Colin Handley suffer and dragged to his knees; but this was the time for fun and rejoicing; Handley's comeuppance would take a few months more.

***

Book 5: The Final Act.

Chapter 1

Four months later, all the legal wrangling had taken place and monies transferred.

Patrick had deposited one million into the accounts of Alex, Jason, Charlie, and Keon. Jess and I would be taken care of in the due course of time, although neither of us needed it; we still had the diamonds, both cut and uncut to dispose of.

Everyone in the house was happy. That was until three o'clock the next morning.

Jessica let out a scream of pain that woke the entire household. She was suffering a pain more intense than she had ever imagined it might have been. Alex called for mother, who immediately sent Patrick to fetch the midwife who lived in the village.

With each contraction came more yells of pain, the like of which I had never heard on any battlefield; poor Jess, what was she going through!

Mother calmed her until the midwife arrived, despite the presence of Alex, who hovered at her side, refusing to leave the room. Jason and I stayed out of the way and made endless cups of coffee in the kitchen.

Two hours later, the stresses and tensions were gone, replaced by an atmosphere of love and joy, when mother came into the kitchen to announce that Jess had given birth to a beautiful and healthy child; a boy.

It was five-thirty. The sun had risen in the clear blue sky, ushering a new family member into our wonderful world of harmony.

Later that day I choked on happiness, as Jess and Alex told me they had decided upon the name Connor; I struggled to hold back the tears as I delicately lifted the new-born child into my arms, knowing that I would do anything to protect my nephew.

Now, not even the millions which we had could bring so much joy to the whole family, and Connor Junior would be the heir to the largest fortune in Australia.

The next few days were consumed by us all wanting to fuss over the baby, still, nevertheless, I continued my ritual of reading the business section of the Telegraph every day. I followed the progress of the Australasia Mining Corporation with a keen interest, as I had invested a million in shares three months earlier and had become one of the major shareholders. Naturally, my stock was purchased by proxy to hide my identity.

Within the first two months, I saw the stock rise to a record level; diamond fever had hit the stock market, and everyone wanted a piece of the action.

The day that the diggers moved in I offloaded my stock, the three-months investment had yielded a 50% return as the shares had gone through the roof: everyone wanting a piece of the action.

The mining corporation had invested millions in equipment, as they ploughed the riverbed into an enormous open cast site, which became deeper and deeper in their fruitless search for diamonds.

The trickle of investors that started selling their worthless stock soon became an avalanche, as they all sought to get rid of their shares in the hopeless diamond mine.

Colin Handley had spent more than $30,000,000 of the shareholders' money, most of whom had now gone bankrupt; they were now calling for the chairperson's head.

Handley, jumped ahead of the game and instantly resigned his position, then a dash to the courts to declare bankruptcy, having placed his Sydney Mansion, his yacht, holiday villas in the Caribbean and Switzerland, his eight-seater Cessna jet and Helicopter all in his wife's name.

How he claimed poverty before the High Court Judge beggared belief, but I suppose they were members of the same 'Old Boy's Club'.

I sat back in my armchair and put the newspaper down; I had read enough for now about the fat pig. It had left me with mixed emotions. Yes, I had made a fortune and in doing so, helped to bring down Colin Handley.

But was he down? Not according to the newspaper reports, so long as he stayed married no one could touch him, and he was bound to have millions stashed away in one of those banks in Switzerland; the taste of victory was already going sour in my mouth.

I knew nothing would ever bring father back, but I would not rest until that bastard had breathed his last.

I walked out onto the patio of my penthouse apartment overlooking the Sydney Theatre House.

I had all the money that I could ever wish for; Jess and Alex were now man and wife, living a blissful life with baby Connor and not a care in the world.

Mother and Patrick living in the cottage by the sea, if you can call an eight-room mansion a cottage. Their days spent happily pottering around or visiting their grandchild.

Aunt Catherine and Daniel's life had changed little; he had successfully laundered all the cash and held the Star of Hopetown locked away in his vault, and Aunt had taken up her pen and started part two of her book.

Jason had bought a small ranch near Longreach, where he and Charlie were breeding a few horses. I had often wondered about the pair of them; but they seemed happy together and what they do in their private lives is not my concern.

All was good in the world, apart from me, living alone with the thoughts of Colin Handley festering in my head.

What was the point? Why couldn't I just let it go?

Committing murder in Australia would be far more difficult than in Mozambique, where we did the deed, then ran.

I really needed to let the whole thing go and wipe Handley from my thoughts; but I couldn't.

I knew in my heart of hearts that I could never rest until the man was dead!

***

Chapter 2

Over the months, there were many articles in the papers about Handley.

Several of the shareholders had grouped together to form a class action against the man; the cocky sod's response was to regularly appear in the media, making sincere promises to repay every dollar.

Mother reminded me it was the same tactic that he had employed all those years ago after the mining disaster. On that occasion, he promised that every family would receive substantial compensation for losing their loved ones.

The thoughts of the man were eating me up; something had to be done.

This was a personal vendetta; it would not be fair to involve the others as their lives were settled. The problem was mine, not theirs, but how would I go about it on my own.

I was neither an assassin nor marksman. Zimbala had been easy; a close-range target and a quick exit.

How would I ever get that close to Handley?

In every photo or TV interview, Davy Buchanan was always seen to be lurking in the background, so I would have to overcome that obstacle first.

The more that I thought about it, the more I realised that this could not be a one-man operation; I needed help.

I had two friends that would never let me down; but was it fair to ask them? Both were nestled in their new world outside of the military; how could I drag them back into the paths of danger?

If I were to approach Alex, then Jessica would kill me, and I wouldn't blame her. No, that was out of the question.

Jason might, he was always looking for the next adventure and Charlie was more than miffed that he had not been party to the African trip.

A trip to Longreach, a few days in the saddle, then casually bring up the subject of murdering someone; what could be easier?

I picked up my phone.

"Hi Jay, how's it going."

Then explained that city life was getting on my nerves. I needed a few days out of Sydney. Fresh air and a chance to commune with nature. Was it ok for me to come up to Queensland and stay awhile?

"Come anytime you like; you don't need an invitation."

"Thanks Jay, I'll fly up and be there tomorrow."

"No problem, let me know the times and I'll meet you at the airport."

Before I could thank him, he added.

"Then you can tell me what you really want, Connor."

Jason may not appear to be the brightest, but he always knew when I was not disclosing the whole truth.

"Ok mate, you're right, there is a little more. I'll explain when I see you."

And we ended the call.

I dashed to my room to pack a case. None of the expensive suits that I had become accustomed to wearing, instead two pairs of jeans, a pile of tee shirts, underwear, and my old leather riding boots.

The plane touched down at noon. Longreach Airport was not too busy, so it was easy to spot Jason and Charlie as I emerged through the arrival gate.

Manly hugs, and then we headed to the carpark.

"Nice wheels," I commented with a smile as Charlie tossed my case into the back of the Ute. Jason had inherited the Toyota that we had bought all those months ago.

"Want to talk now or save it until we've had a cold one." Jason asked over his shoulder.

Charlie had taken the front passenger seat, and why shouldn't he? He was his own man, and no longer worked for our family.

"A beer sounds good; it's nothing that cannot wait."

It was my first visit to their stud farm, only thirty or forty acres, set on the green slopes of the Range. A large, traditional lapboard farmhouse with a selection of stables, barns, and outhouses. Several paddocks with an assortment of horses and foals.

Charlie proudly pointing everything out to me as we approached through the gates and along the drive to the house front.

We were greeted by Keon, who introduced two of his older nephews, who were employed as stable lads.

I looked at what they had achieved with their newly found wealth and immediately felt the pangs of guilt.

It was an idyllic scene of contentedness. Jason and Charlie were so easy together, the joy and happiness was clear for all to see. And I had come here to ask Jason to risk all that he had, just to satisfy my lust for revenge.

I should have asked him to take me straight back to the Airport; but I did not.

Where was my conscience, my sense of right and wrong?

"Another beer?" offered Jay, as the six of us sat around the fire pit and Keon fetched out the sausages to cook.

"Cheers, how can I say no? This beats my life in Sydney. I can't remember the last time we cooked snags over an open fire."

The two nephews were keen to hear all about Sydney; Longreach with its population of less than three thousand was the furthest they had ever travelled, but I was sure that one day they would visit one of the big cities.

"So, what's important enough to drag you all the way to Queensland." Jason asked once we had all finished eating.

"Nothing at all, I just needed a change of scenery and a chance to clear my head." I was genuinely enjoying being with them, but wishing that I had stayed away.

I felt myself sliding back into the old habit of telling lies.

I had decided I would stay a few days, then return to New South Wales: taking my evil thoughts with me.

The few days of relaxation with Jason and the others were terrific – but I spent my nights in torment, as my longing to permanently wipe the smile off the fat face of Colin Handley increased.

I knew Jason would never refuse a request from me, given that his life of bliss and recently acquired fortune had been generated through our relationship – but no, I could not ask him to risk it all.

I had been there for five nights and did not want to overstay my welcome; it was time for me to leave.

After breakfast, I informed Jason that I would return to Sydney and requested that one of them drive me to the airport.

"Thanks for the warm welcome, Jay. You and the guys have been great. I feel refreshed and ready to return to city life."

"It's been good to see you, but if you don't mind me saying mate, you look crap."

"Sorry Jay?" I asked indignantly.

"Don't get me wrong, it's been great having you, but refreshed and rested? Well, you don't look it. Have you slept at all since you arrived?"

"Of course, I have; I feel good. I've just had a lot on my mind." I put on a confident smile and sipped my coffee.

"That's a load of bollocks. How many years have I known you? Enough to know when you're lying. So, what is it? And the truth this time, you're supposed to be my mate, so tell me what it is."

Jason had me cornered. There was nowhere to run and hide; so I told him the full story of how I had plotted to bring down Colin Handley; and appeared to have succeeded.

Then forced to watch the slimy toad's face on the television as he wriggled and slid his way out of his hole.

Making promises he had no intentions of keeping, just as he had when my father and the others were killed in the mine all those years ago.

I had lusted for revenge, and that feeling had to be satisfied or I would go crazy. The only thing that would fulfil my desirers, would be to see Handley the Mining Magnate buried in a hole of his own.

By the end of my telling, I sat with head in hands and tears running down my face.

A strong muscular arm gently placed around my shoulder, and soft tender words whispered into my ear.

"Did you ever doubt that I would help a colleague? You only had to ask. Now forget going home. We need time to think this one through."

***

Chapter 3

We spent the next two weeks collecting everything that we knew about Colin Handley; every news item, press release, interview; of which there were many, as he continued to duck and dive both the shareholders and the authorities.

Both Jason and I agreed that this was an operation that would not include either Alex or Jess. We considered employing the services of Mad Mike Simpson, then ditched that idea.

We suspected that he might have been a Mason, and felt certain that Handley must have been, in order to have escaped the authorities for all these years, with his endless dodgy dealings.

Yes, they could have been in the same Old Boys club, so kept our circle as small as possible.

We were down to the "how, where and when"? Having agreed that the best method would be an assassin's bullet.

Handley still resided in the Sydney mansion owned by his wife, close to where he moored his luxury yacht.

Access to the building would be most unwise, CCTV cameras everywhere, and he still employed that oaf of a bodyguard, Davy Buchanan. He was Handley's pet Rottweiler and would be daft enough to take a bullet for his master.

No, the house was out of the question.

That left the Helicopter or the Yacht; and as much as I wanted the man dead, blowing the chopper out of the sky or sinking the yacht could mean considerable collateral damage, which neither of us were prepared to live with.

Our options were running out. It would have to be a long-range shot from a marksman's gun; a weapon which we did not have. Our only firearms being the two shot guns Jason used for killing vermin around the farm.

"How the hell are we going to get our hands on a sniper's rifle? Maybe we'll have to risk buying in another favour from Mad Mike after all." I was resigned to the fact that he was the only one that could get his hands on an appropriate weapon to carry out the job.

"Or maybe not." Jason's face reddened. "About the Remington; I've a small confession to make."

Jason then admitted that he had done a deal with Dominique; we had all witnessed him dropping the weapons into the sea but had not noticed the fishing line attached to the gun case. There it remained, being dragged along in our wake until after the inspection by the Border Force.

"It's a beautiful gun and perfect for the task."

I could not argue with that; Jay was the expert.

Was it good luck, or an act of God? I did not know; therefore I took it as a sign that what we were doing was fated. Handley had to die!

From the information that we had gathered, most weekends he liked to pose around the Harbour aboard his yacht, making him an easy target.

"One clear shot from a passing dinghy should do the trick. How close would you need to be?" I asked.

"Six hundred metres should be ok, but with all the bobbing about, maybe three or four hundred." He confidently replied.

So we decided Jason and Charlie would accompany me to Sydney, and if all went well, my final act of vengeance would be complete, and my agitated mind finally allowed to rest.

The following morning Keon dropped the three of us at a private airfield; I had chartered a light aircraft, knowing that the pilot would not be too inquisitive about our cargo.

We were travelling light, with only one piece of luggage each. Jason had dismantled the Remington, and packed it into his holdall, along with half a dozen rounds of ammunition.

It was a bumpy take-off in the small twin-engine plane, and Charlie's first time in the air. Jason's comforting words did not reassure him. He clung onto his seat, in the belief that if God had wanted us to fly, he would have given us wings.

A few hours later, we were flying over the southern section of the Great Dividing Range; it would not be long before the anxious Charlie had his feet back on the ground.

We landed on a small farm airstrip close to Dubbo; the last 200 kilometres to Sydney would be made by road.

"Bloody hell, how much did you pay for this pad?" asked Jason in amazement as we entered my penthouse apartment.

"More than enough, but I'm already thinking that I'd rather swap it with your place. This is just a box with great views over the city; it's not a home," I admitted. "There are six bedrooms, so help yourselves." Then added, "They are all doubles."

"Cheers, mate." Jay gave me an embarrassed smile.

"What's for tucker? I'm starving," added Charlie, attempting to change the subject of sleeping arrangements."

"The fridge is empty, and I don't cook, so when you're showered and sorted we will eat out." It was my turn to feel humiliated; I was not accustomed to having visitors. Apart from the odd one-nighter that I had picked up from a bar or club, these were the only two friends that I have ever invited to stay.

We had a pleasant evening. I skipped my usual restaurants, and we settled with Charlie's request and found a Burger Bar.

That night, as I lay alone in my bed, I realised how sad my life had become. I should be happy. I had as much money that anyone could dream of having; yet my world was only fuelled by thoughts of revenge, and in the whole of Sydney, there was not a soul that I could call a friend.

***

Chapter 4

The next morning it was an expedition to Point Piper Marina, to rent ourselves a small boat.

When we arrived, the marina was not what I had expected to see; instead, it was rows upon rows of expensive, flashy looking yachts. Their owners would most likely be members at the adjacent Royal Motor Yacht Club.

But it was not a totally wasted journey, as we spotted the 'Major Miner', a beautiful craft that had once belonged to Colin Handley, now the property of his wife.

The three of us took a casual stroll, posing as innocent tourists admiring all these impressive boats. All the time making mental notes; looking for a secluded spot where Jason would have a clear line of sight, seemingly there was none to be found.

We concluded we would revert to our original plan and went in search of a boat to hire.

I struck it lucky at the Double Bay Marina on the other side of the Point. The boat was not much bigger than the average tinny, a single out-board motor, but most importantly a small canopy, which Jason could use as cover whilst making the shot.

On the Friday morning, I approached the owner and explained that I had two friends visiting for a long weekend. They were both keen anglers, so we hoped to get a bit of fishing in before they left.

"How long will you want it, mate?"

"Two or three days, it depends on what we catch."

"Try the far side of the point. If you avoid the shipping lanes, you'll find plenty of fish there." He helpfully suggested, then looked at me thoughtfully. "Two or three days, you say, then I'll want a hefty deposit, and payment in advance."

I smiled and pulled out a large wad of notes, counted out what he had asked for, and put it in his hand.

"Cheers. I'll fill the petrol tank; you can pick her up after six in the morning." He said as he returned my smile and asked no further questions.

We picked the boat up at six-thirty. The forecast for the day was good, but as we motored away from the jetty, the temperature had only just reached double figures.

"Bloody hell, man, doesn't it get any warmer than this?"

It was another first for Charlie. They were forecasting thirty degrees at his home; he had never been so far south or so cold in his life.

"Don't worry, it will be twenty-four degrees by lunchtime," I reassured him.

We slowly rounded the Point, and the Point Piper Marina came into view. When we were a hundred metres away, I cut the motor and we drifted whilst we unwrapped our equipment; our three bags, two of which contained the rods, the other the Remington.

Our rucksacks contained a flask of coffee, packs of pre-wrapped sandwiches, a bunch of bananas and a pair of binoculars. The bucket of bait was just for show; we had no intention of attempting to catch any fish; only the Fat Cat from the Major Miner when he showed his face.

At midday, there was some movement.

A limo pulled up at the end of the jetty. Davy Buchanan got out of the driver's door, then opened the rear doors for Colin Handley and his wife.

The pair swanned along the jetty as though they owned it. Well, by that I mean she sashayed, and he waddled, the fat pig! Then they boarded their yacht and were joined five minutes later by Buchanan, after he had parked the car and lugged their bags aboard.

This was it. Any moment they would come our way. Charlie and I continued the pretence of fishing, while Jason slid down under the canopy and reassembled the Remington. He snuggled into a comfortable position, adjusted the sights, and put a round into the breach; our marksman was ready.

Patiently we waited, and waited, and waited; two hours went by.

The only activity had been his wife sunning herself on the upper deck and Buchanan running in and out to refill her glass of bubbly. My mind started wandering as the time dragged, and my binoculars focused on his wife. And in all fairness, as trophies went, Mrs Handley didn't look bad in her scanty bikini. Then my lurid thoughts were interrupted by Jason.

"Is he ever going to take that fucking boat out? I'm getting cramp down here and dying for a piss."

"Sorry Jay, I might have been a little premature. It's time to put the gun away. It doesn't look as though they're going anywhere today; we'll try again tomorrow."

Two tugs and the motor started. Then I reluctantly navigated back to the Double Bay Marina, where we moored in our allotted berth, and took a taxi back to my apartment.

"What's to say that Handley will take his yacht out tomorrow?" asked Jason, after he had screwed the top off his beer.

"Nothing really, but why spend the day on the boat? If he has no intentions of taking it out, it just doesn't make sense."

"You're not wrong man, he must be here for a reason; but it doesn't seem to be fishing or sailing." Added Charlie.

They were both right. His wife had spent the day sunning herself, but Handley had hardly shown his face; I was sure that he hadn't come aboard just so that she could top up her tan.

I opened my laptop and googled up Colin Handley for the hundredth time. There was a new headline on his Facebook page. This Sunday, he was handing out the awards at the Royal Yacht Club.

"So that's it, he'll be lording it in front of his pals on Sunday evening. I think we can forget it this weekend." It really pissed me off; all this waste of effort, and for what!

"Don't be so defeatist, Connor. Just think it through for a moment. The Yacht Club is less than 200 metres from where they are moored; even a fat bastard like Handley can walk that far for God's sake."

"What are you saying?"

"What I'm saying, Connor, is that I won't get a better chance of a clear shot than when he comes staggering back from the Club."

"But that could be at midnight, and pitch black."

"Exactly, my friend. I'll have the cover of darkness and the advantage of night vision on my sights. It'll be a piece of cake; trust me."

"You're the expert Jay. It's only eight o'clock. I suggest we should head back down there for another reconnoitre."

We abandoned our drinks and took the lift to the carpark in the basement.

"Which one's yours?" asked Charlie.

I smiled and pressed the remote on my keyring; a double bleep and the lights of a black Porsche came on.

"You flashy bastard; has Jessica got one of these as well?" he asked as I opened the doors.

"Strangely not; she still insists on driving that old Beetle of hers. This one's only designed for two, so you'll have to squeeze into the back seat." And I slid the driver's seat forward so that he could climb in.

Two minutes later, we were racing through the streets of Sydney, heading for Point Piper and one step closer to fulfilling my dream.

We parked on the road opposite the marina, from there we could see the twenty or so yachts moored either side of the jetty, most of which were in darkness, just a few with lights on, including the Major Miner, where the occupants would sleep overnight. The lighting was minimal, just enough to illuminate the walkway. A large electronically operated gate at the entrance, with a CCTV camera above it.

Jason took out the night scope from his jacket pocket and surveyed the area, and grinned as he replaced it.

"As I said, a piece of cake."

"So what's the plan Jay?" I asked.

Jason then laid out his plans.

We would return in our little boat tomorrow evening under the cover of darkness, board one of the unoccupied yachts, and with his night scope and silencer, it should only take him one shot to blow Handley's brains out.

Good plans always sounded so easy. There was absolutely nothing that could go wrong.

***

Chapter 5

On Sunday morning, I sent Jason and Charlie out shopping.

For our night operation, we would need to purchase suitable clothing, namely black sweaters, and balaclavas. It also gave the pair of them a little private time together while I refocussed my attention on our target; I must admit that it was becoming somewhat of an obsession with me.

On the gossip section of Sunday's paper, I read that Mrs Handley had placed the mansion on the market; the asking price – ten million. There were also rumours that she had been enquiring about properties in the Bahamas.

It was obvious to anyone with half a brain that the Handleys were preparing to cut and run; so much for his promises of repaying the shareholders every last dollar!

It was mid-afternoon when the boys returned, armed with several shopping bags.

"Did you get everything we needed?" I asked inquisitively.

"Sure." And Jason tossed me one bag that contained the sweaters and balaclavas. "Oh, the other bags? Charlie got a bit carried away; a few presents for the boys at home."

"Why not? And did you have a nice lunch?" I asked, giving him a suspicious, knowing look.

"Yes, and don't look so worried; diet Coke, no alcohol," he replied.

Six o'clock, we left the penthouse and drove to the Double Bay Marina, untied our boat, and slowly putted our way around the point to Pipers.

It was now seven-thirty. We could see the lights of the Royal Motor Yacht Club as we entered the marina and could hear a band playing and the noise of loud voices echoing across the still water; the event was in full swing.

Alongside the Major Miner, there were five yachts in complete darkness; we chose the one in the middle, tied on to the ladder at the stern and silently climbed aboard.

Once we were confident that this vessel and the ones on either side were deserted, Jason positioned himself on the top deck. It was perfect; he had a clear line of sight from the gate to Handley's yacht.

He reassembled the Remington, attached the silencer and telescopic sights. All we had to do was wait quietly, one clean shot, back onto our little boat and away.

What could be easier?

At half ten, the noise spilt out of the club and onto the jetty as the guests left the building.

"Heads up guys, it could be any moment now," I excitedly urged.

The security light above the gate flashed on as a couple staggered through the gate. Jason levelled his gun at them; it was not Handley, so Jason relaxed his grip. The two partygoers made their way to a yacht on the other side of the Jetty, and the light went out.

Ten minutes later it flashed on again; this time it was the Handley's, who were drunkenly staggering along towards their yacht.

It was only a 50-metre shot, the bullet passing straight through his head; his wife's dress splattered with his brains.

She let out a blood-curdling scream that echoed around the marina, then recoiled from his body as it toppled to the floor.

We had done it!

I leapt into the air with elation. At last I had achieved the revenge I lusted for: Colin Handley was dead!

This was not the time to stand and gloat over my success. Now we had to make good our escape. I climbed onto our boat; Jason hurriedly dismantled the Remington and rammed it into his bag while Charlie held the rope; waiting for Jason to jump aboard before casting off.

"Quick Jay, we've got company," Charlie shouted.

Buchanan had appeared, barefoot in his shorts and carrying an automatic pistol. He paused for an instant by Handley's body, then sprinted in our direction.

"Jay, get a move on," I urged; but too late.

It only took one leap, and the giant of a man was aboard the yacht and raced to the stern.

The first shot caught Jason on the shoulder, the second two on Charlie's back. But before he could aim the next in my direction, he was knocked off balance, as the wounded Jason lunged his body into Buchanan.

It should have been a total mismatch, Jason a mere five-foot-five, against this Goliath of a man who still had a gun in his hand.

With nothing to use as a weapon, Jay drove his thumbs deeply into his adversaries' eyes, and the blood came spurting out.

Buchanan dropped the gun, and screamed in agony, his hands clutching where his eyes had been, and the blood running through his fingers.

Jason pulled back from the man, snatched up the gun, and discharged the remaining rounds into the body. He stood astride the corpse, then spat at Buchanan's face before we rolled it into the water. We removed the balaclavas and cradled Charlie's body down into the boat.

Charlie was unconscious. I feared the worse but could not summon up the courage to ask as he lay in Jason's arms.

I drove our little boat as fast as it would go; I needed to put some distance between us and the Piper Marina before the police descended.

The only witness was the wife, Kylie Handley. But she had been so drunk that the police could hardly rely upon her version of events. Anyway, what had she actually seen; three men in black wearing balaclava masks. No, I would not have to worry about Mrs Handley.

We rounded the Point in silence, and at last I felt I could take a sigh of relief. In the darkness, I could not see Jason's face, as he held Charlie close to his.

"How's he doing?" I cautiously asked Jason, who had not spoken since we made our getaway.

"He is not." And he turned his face towards me. In the half-light, I could see the tears streaming down his face.

Jason's injury had been superficial, but the two bullets that had struck Charlie in the back had gone straight through his chest, killing him outright.

I cut the motor, and we drifted. I had known him since I was thirteen-years old, and he was a good friend; I knew to Jason however he was much, much more.

Feelings of panic, feelings of guilt; what had I done?

I had fulfilled my dreams, but in doing so had destroyed the lives of two good men.

We sat in silence aimlessly drifting, neither knowing what to say to the other; there were no words that could describe the way I felt at that moment; I wished I were the one that was dead.

Jason's tears dripping down onto his lover's face; unable to look me in the eye. If he wanted to kill me; then I could not have blamed him. I deserved no less.

Eventually, he broke the silence.

"What are we going to do?"

A strange question, to which I had no answer. Did he mean about the murders, or Charlie's body?

"What are we going to do with Charlie?" he asked again.

"I don't know," I pathetically replied.

"Well, we can neither take him home, nor report his death to the police." He wiped his face with the discarded balaclava, then tossed it into the water. "We have very few options. Ideally, I would wish to take him back to his family and bury him on the ranch. But that is an impossibility, I think that the best we can do is to bury him here; at sea."

Jason had always been the one in our group to take the pragmatic view, although I knew whatever decision that we came to would leave him scarred for life.

We reverently stripped his body, removing every item of identification. I then attached the small boat's anchor to his ankles.

Neither of us were religious men; few are that have experienced the atrocities of war. But we knelt either side of his naked body and prayed silently.

Jason; for the soul of his lost love.

Me; for all my sins, vanity, anger, and lusting for the revenge that had caused this tragedy.

Jason kissed him for the last time, and we eased the body into the ocean. He then opened his bag, and piece by piece dropped all the parts of his precious Remington into the water.

***

Chapter 6

Four months later, I was not surprised to hear that Jason had sold the Stud Farm and returned to Brisbane; and if everything that I was told was true, he was rapidly burning through his fortune on drink and drugs.

I was fairing no better; despite my wealth, I still could not form any relationships; I had no friends and desperately missed my family.

The flashy lifestyle in Sydney was taking its toll. Besides the alcohol, I could now afford the high-end drugs, and became a Coke Head.

Strangely, my only salvation was losing myself in books and reading the newspapers.

The widow Kylie Handley had not grieved for long; it was reported in the papers that she had bought a property in the Caribbean and was planning to move as soon as she had sold the mansion in Sydney.

I was bored and had nothing better to do, so rang the agents and arranged a viewing.

The property was bigger that any private dwelling that I had ever been inside. It was once owned by the Governor General back in the mid-eighteen hundreds. A fine stone-built structure with an East and West wing and housed a magnificent library.

My thoughts immediately went to mother; she would love a library of this size and splendour.

As I was being shown around, these thoughts kept developing; the West wing would be perfect for Jessica, Alex, and baby Connor.

There were so many rooms, even an annex at the rear; that would be perfect for Jason, and we would all be able to keep an eye on him and support him through his grieving process.

Yes, the house was perfect.

The next day, I called them all together for a second viewing. They were over the moon; they thought it a wonderful idea.

I made Kylie Handley an offer that was accepted.

A month later, we all moved in; the wealthiest family in Australia, living in this wonderful mansion.

My life was perfect.

I had Righted all the Wrongs, Avenged all the Wrong doers, and my Ducks were all in a row under one roof; nothing in the world could make me happier.

*****

Epilogue

"Connor." The Chair of the Board sighed, looked up from the notes, removed her spectacles and stared me in the face.

"Connor Malloy." She paused and lowered her tone.

"Connor, it has been two years since you came to the hospital, and still we see no improvement. Until you accept the realities and come out of this world of fantasy, you will remain where you are."

What was the stupid woman talking about; my name is Connor van Vuuren.

"I'm Connor van Vuuren, not Malloy; you stupid bitch!" I screamed as I stood and kicked away my chair in frustration.

"Sit down Connor, or I'll have the orderlies put you back in your restraints."

One of them stepped forward; righted the chair and pulled me back onto the seat.

"Settle down mate," he whispered into my ear. "They are only trying to help."

I took a deep breath, lifted my head, and looked at the panel who were sat in a row behind the bench, all staring straight at me.

"Connor, I have read all the medical and social reports; your impressive list of commendations speak for themselves." She gave a sad sigh. "But, but you cannot go through life pretending to be who you are not. Lieutenant van Vuuren died in your arms six years ago, and there is no diamond; the Star of Hopetown just does not exist."

"No! You're not listening," I screamed in frustration as the tears ran down my face. "Everything I said is true, you're just not listening to me."

Jessica, Alex, mother, and Patrick. Jason, Charlie, and Keon; they were not just some imaginary characters, they were my family.

And, what was wrong with them? Why had they not come forward and spoken out for me?

"Orderlies, take Connor back to his room," instructed the Chair, "We will review your case in another six months."

"No, Ma'am! Please," I shouted back over my shoulder; the tears still streaming down my cheeks. But there was no response; the board just sat in silence as I was taken back to my padded room.

As I sat on the bed wiping my eyes, a thought came to me.

If I could get my hands on the diamond, I could buy my way out of this hellhole!

I reached for a pen and paper, and started to set out another plan……………

THE END

The Authors

This story is a collaboration between
Michael Claxton and
Rosalie Enstrom

Rosalie is an award-winning writer, who specialises in Memoirs, her titles include –
"Flight to Freedom", "The Silent Knight", "Harry", and her recently released "Deprivation and Abuse"

Michael, a retired detective from the Metropolitan Police in London, writes in the Crime Genre and his other titles include -
"Killing Time" An anthology of 12 Murder Stories.
"Redemption or Revenge" and "No Game" in the Murders London Series.

Visit their websites at-
www.RosalieEnstromBooks.com
www.michaelclaxtonauthor.com

Author's Notes - This work is a complete fiction, any resemblance to anyone either alive or dead from Australia or South Africa is purely coincidental.

Manufactured by Amazon.com.au
Sydney, New South Wales, Australia